ODD EVENING
AT THE
HOUSE OF GREASE

BY JOHN MONTÉT

FOR DANI

Odd Evening at the House of Grease
Copyright © 2013
By John Montét
Published by Drawquarter Press

www.OddEvening.com

ISBN-13: 978-0615792132
ISBN-10: 0615792138

ODD EVENING
AT THE
HOUSE OF GREASE

Chapter 1

THE WORLD TURNED SIDEWAYS as it came into focus. Hazy evergreen trees thrust from distant vertical hills into the cloudy left-hand sky. The ground stretched upward into the air, still holding tight to the dusty sand-colored gravel of the pot-holed parking lot outside Lucky's Bar. It was the gravel biting into his cheek that finally brought Michael Chord back to reality. It was either that or the size fourteen Caterpillar work boot firmly planted on the side of his face.

He hadn't been unconscious for long, he knew, though he wasn't sure what exactly had put him in such a prone position. It could be that he simply hadn't won the fight. It could be that someone blindsided him. He certainly wasn't feeling especially sharp after such a long ride. He decided to just not move for the moment. Waiting might give his head a chance to clear.

He took mental stock of himself. There was a deep pounding in his head, though not from the boot's attempt to make him one with the crushed rock. It was an insistent throbbing just above the back of his neck. It meant the blindsided theory was correct. It meant he was just stupid.

Even through the size-fourteen, Chord could hear muffled laughter - nearby and obnoxious. That was instructive. It meant that there were several people in the parking lot. His blurry eyes could just make out the shapes of a few of them. Their silhouettes merged with the trees at the edge of the parking lot.

His head clearing, Michael Chord started to plan. The first order of business was to get out from under the boot. If he could get what's-his-name to let up for a moment, it would be enough. He tried a little fish-faced moan.

Bill Ullage, the owner of thoroughly worn and somewhat dusty Caterpillar work boots looked down in mock surprise.

"Easy Rider lives!" he announced to a round of approving laughter. He shifted his weight to lean just a little heavier on Chord's head. Bill looked up, guffawing with his fans.

Chord felt the pressure ebb just a bit as the laughter increased. It was exactly what he needed.

Sliding his face against the gravel, Chord spun himself sideways along the ground in a 180-degree arc, scraping his cheek painfully, but freeing his head. As he spun, he lifted his leg past Ullage, then drove back hard in a scissor kick, planting his own Red Wing motorcycle boot into Bill's sternum with the force of a wind-milling donkey. Ullage coughed a deep "oof" as the blow drove him to the ground, his head smacking the gravel hard.

Chord quickly spun to his feet, looking to drive a

dark-heeled finishing blow into the body of his attacker, but there was no need. Bill was out cold, his head deep inside a pothole. His glazed eyes stared up under partially closed lids into the unmoving sky.

Chord turned to the spectators. There were only three men. Two of them wore the baseball caps, tee shirts, and jeans that made up the general uniform of the younger Rhotic County residents. The third looked more Minnesotan in a plaid over shirt and brown pants. None of them moved. They simply looked first to their prone friend, then back to him.

"Well?" Chord said.

Still no one moved.

"Fine," he said. "You clean it up." Chord wiped at his scratched face as he started across the parking lot back toward Lucky's bar, trying not to stagger. Swirls and splotches of light still played behind his eyes, but the ringing was starting to fade. He hoped he looked better than he felt. Maybe the rest of his beer was still sitting on the bar. Maybe it was still cold.

Half an hour earlier, a road-weary Michael Chord had ridden down through the forested hills on the northern side of the Mismate River Valley. It had been a long, but enjoyable ride. He couldn't resist rolling back the throttle into the deep swoops and through the small valleys between the hills. He chose this route at the last minute specifically because of the curves. It was as if they were made for a biker's soul. It also helped that it was far from the normal interstate traffic routes. There were decidedly less highway patrolmen on this route.

At the bottom of the last hill sat the small town of Clements. Chord was following highway 324 as it slithered down the hill and through the town at steep angles to form the main street through Clements. The hills colluded with police to form very effective speed traps on each side of town.

Fortunately, Chord was only doing forty as he passed the speed limit sign at the bottom of the hill. Officer Neil Clark, sitting in his cruiser, watched the Triumph Speedmaster pass, glanced at the radar readout, then went back to reading his book.

Chord had been riding the entire morning, having left The Cities not long after midnight. The case of swamp-ass he'd developed after crossing the state line was reaching a level verging on bayou. A break was sorely needed. He scanned the street, darting his eyes from one side of the street to the other until they locked onto the sign over Lucky's. Its rounded corners and burger-with-the-works-shaped relief was a welcoming site, even if the meat looked a little odd. It may have just been the fading paint. Regardless, it made a much more inviting picture than the line of newer pickups and SUV's parked across the street in front of Heaven's Kitchen Supper Club. Lucky's was more his kind of place.

Chord dropped the kickstand of the flat black motorcycle and swung off the bike in a single practiced motion. A glance at the sky told him that the clouds, while dreary, were not about to burst. There was no wind. There wouldn't be rain - at least not yet. The distant ozone smell of a storm ticked a note in the back of his biker brain, but for now, his pack and gear were safe. The same held true for the gems, his cargo, perfectly protected in the hidden compartment in the Triumph's frame. Chord gave the spot a quick glance, turned, and walked into Lucky's.

Ralph Doless captained the helm of Lucky's Bar for the past twelve years. The bar remained a staple in Clements for a little over a century, though under a string of different names. The first proprietor converted what was the newly defunct Clements City Bank into an eating-house. He named the establishment after his dog. Ten years later Sparky's Place nearly burned to the ground.

From then on, the bar's fate was inextricably tied to its name. The next owner reconstructed the bar, turning it into the River Café. This lasted for another ten years before a burst pipe in the ceiling driving the owner out of business. A similar thing happened to the Water's Edge when the sewer backed up a decade later. And so it was that Blazing Hearth, Danny's Sinkhole Saloon, Wild Bill's Buffett, Four Closures (few noticed the misspelling of "Clovers"), Gladys' Revenge, Not This Time Diner, and The Last Chance Pub all passed by without anyone noticing the correlation. Such was not the case with Ralph Doless. Irony being one of Ralph's strong suits, he was resolute in his decision to use the name Lucky's Bar. The strategy seemed to be working. He'd gone past the normal decade-long run. The bank was happy; the customers were happy. Still, Ralph couldn't escape the thought that fate was simply two years overdue.

Lucky's was a dark place, even at noon. The sweet smell of cigars clung to the wooden chairs and tables, though Ralph banned smoking well before the state law. Rich, worn wooden paneling soaked up the glow from the four neon signs. Lights inset in the ornate nautical carvings above the massive mirror behind the bar only deepened the shadows in the wood. The grill at the front of the joint gave the large front window above it a sepia tint.

Lucky's saving grace was the digital jukebox set on the wall next to the electronic dartboard. The company that installed it hadn't been back since receiving a $250 speeding ticket on their way into town. Ralph's nephew managed to hack the machine and install Ralph's extensive music collection. Patrons could be treated to Frank Sinatra, Joe Satriani, Hank Williams, Kenny Burrell, Motorhead, and John Lee Hooker all in the same evening. The machine remained stuck on random since the nephew went to college.

Ralph was wearing his ubiquitous, off-white cable knit sweater, polishing a glass, when Chord walked in wearing a leather jacket and severely windblown hair. He paused to look around for a moment, squinted out the window at the bike he parked out front then took a seat at the near end of the bar.

Ralph walked to stand across from the man and said nothing, the question being implicit.

The biker leaned his elbows on the bar and glanced up at Ralph.

"Beer?" Chord asked.

"You'll have to be more specific," Ralph said.

"Bud Light."

"Don't carry it."

"Really? It's the single most popular beer in the United States. Who doesn't carry Bud Light?"

"We don't. It tastes like crap. If I wouldn't drink it, I won't serve it."

Chord looked at Ralph a little closer; the hint of a smile crept across the biker's face.

"Well then, I'll have a glass of whatever beer you normally drink."

"I don't drink."

"What? But you do serve beer, right."

"Of course," Ralph said. "This is a bar. But, I don't drink. It leads to bad luck. I serve the beer I would drink if I were to drink beer."

"And that would be?" Chord's scarcely hidden smile was more pronounced and Ralph found himself starting to like this guy.

"How about a Samuel Smith's? They make a very nice oatmeal stout."

"Too strong," Chord said shaking his head slightly. "I'm on two wheels."

"A nut brown ale then," Ralph didn't phrase it as a question. He just headed to the large, antique, converted icebox he used as a refrigerator and pulled out a bottle. Neither man said a word while Ralph popped the cap and poured it into a glass. Ralph walked back to the front end of the bar and set the glass, along with the bottle, in front of his new patron.

"Expertly done," the biker said. "I appreciate a good pour." He reached for the glass and took a pull. "Very good."

"Ralph."

"Chord. Good to meet you."

"You know," Chord proffered, "they say that a beer is commonality. It is a drink as old as the ancients and as refined as the most cherished painting. What was it Thomas Jefferson said? 'Beer is proof that there is a god and he loves us very much.'"

"It was Ben Franklin, actually," Ralph said. He pointed to a sign on the opposite wall. "You almost got it right."

Chord turned, looked at the sign, and then turned back to Ralph. "An expert in beer and its culture, yet you don't drink."

"That's about the size of it." Ralph picked up empty glass number two and started polishing it.

"Interesting," Chord said, going back to his beer.

Ralph did indeed like this guy. The same could not be said for the guy who just lost the pool game at the back of the bar. Ralph realized the oaf had been staring at Chord's back, whispering to his companions. Ralph moved toward the "Crowd Control Policy" he kept in a sling under the bar.

Bill Ullage could be such an asshole when he didn't win.

CHAPTER 2

JAIRUS DISHOME WOKE UP earlier than usual, though he wasn't sure why. It could be that nagging itch in his nose. When he'd lain down, he did so as discreetly as possible, taking care to not be noticed by the patrol cruiser parked in the lot of the old rail station across from the grain bin - his resting spot. He half expected the sheriff to burst in like a Hun and to provoke him awake with a Billy club. Instead, he was roused from his slumber by something brushing his nose.

"Rhapsode, get your tail out of my face," he said without opening his eyes. "I'm trying to sleep. That by-child sheriff hasn't even left yet."

"By-child?"

Jairus slowly lifted one eyelid. If his trusty hound had suddenly learned to talk, his life truly had changed for the worse.

Rhapsode sat staring at him, a canine smile on his face showing that he was really enjoying himself. Sheriff Neil Clark was standing next to the dog, scratching Rhapsode's ears. Jairus noticed a long strand of grass in the sheriff's hand.

"Blast you, you sombolist interruptus." Jairus pulled the torn canvas more tightly around him and tried to pretend to go back to sleep. "Et tu, Rhapsode?"

"Jairus-" the sheriff started.

"Dr. Dishome to you." Jairus kept his eyes closed.

"Dr. Dishome, then. You know you can't stay here. I'm sure I'm going to get a complaint from Mr. Harris once he finds out you're sleeping in his grain house."

"And just how, pray tell, is he going to find out?" Jairus opened an eye again. "Will you sing the pigeon's song?"

"No. I won't mention anything unless he asks. But I'm sure he is going to assume it wasn't the Melbostad boys who painted 'Dim Sparrow Sparrow' on the wall."

"Dum Spiro Spero, Sheriff."

"I see. And what does that mean exactly?" The sheriff squinted at the lettering above Jairus' head and sniffed. "Wait. What is that written in? It isn't..."

"Axel grease, yes." Jairus could see he wasn't going to get to sleep again. He slowly sat up. "It means 'while I breathe, I hope'. Perhaps I grew a bit maudlin last night."

"Perhaps with a little help from Stagger and Jags Liquors?" Rhapsode was sniffing at the lip of an empty bottle of Pappy Van Winkle's bourbon. The dog apparently figured if no one was going to scratch him, a light buzz would suffice.

Clark knew only rumors regarding Jairus' past. It was said that he was a disgraced professor of history at one of the three state universities; the stories placed him in each depending on the telling.

As to the cause of the disgrace, the speculation ranged from running an underground methamphetamine lab ("obviously that much rat killer will get to anyone..."), to setting up wild orgies with the coeds. Others said he was an ex-military man whose mind was shattered in Viet Nam after a buddy threw himself on a grenade to save Jairus as he was squatting in the bush to relieve himself. The trauma supposedly caused Jairus to take far too many laxatives in an effort to speed his necessities, which "does something to a man, you know." (Every version of this story includes that his buddy lived, but lost a testicle in the incident.)

The fact was that Clark never had cause to investigate which of these rumors may have been true. Jairus didn't cause any real trouble in town. Instead, he spent an inordinate amount of time in the town library - time, which Jairus said, he spent in an effort to get out of the rain, regardless of the weather. When Clark inquired if Jairus was a nuisance, he was told that Jairus was a key reason they were able to keep their circulation up. He also knew so much about the library that some of the more regular patrons would use Jairus as a verbal book index, though a rather acerbic one.

"Perhaps the local libation emporium played a part. But one can hardly lay blame upon their doorstep, can one?" Jairus said to the sheriff. For the lawman's part, he was trying hard not to 'loom'.

Jairus turned to address his dog. "Rhapsode, leave it! You know how you get when you are in the spirits."

"How does he get?"

"Contrite. It's insufferable."

Sheriff Clark looked down at the golden, longhaired dog. He was really in very good shape for the dog of a homeless man.

"What kind of dog is he, Jairus- I mean, Doctor?"

"He's the best specimen of a golden retriever you will ever likely see, my good man. Man's best friend, when there isn't another man around."

Rhapsode looked up at Jairus. One would have thought a man who claimed to have a Ph.D. would have known a Nova Scotia Duck Tolling Retriever when he saw one. Since you really can't tell a human anything, the dog went back to trying to lick the last dregs out of the bottle.

"You know you can't stay here, Professor. It's trespassing. Why don't you go over to June's Place? I'm sure-"

"Out of the question. That pontifical wench does nothing but insult her patrons. You'd think she'd be more matriarchal as the mistress of a flophouse. She called me saturnine!"

"I know. You've said so before. But that was years ago. June's a very nice lady and the Nap 'N' Breakkers is a very nice bed and breakfast. It's not a flophouse. She won't be busy until the leaves turn and the leaf peepers arrive, so I'm sure she will make up a room for you again. It's only a mile and a half up the hill. I'll give you a ride."

Jairus looked up at the sheriff. He sighed and then held out a weathered glove for assistance. The officer obliged and helped him to his feet.

"I know she's a nice young woman. I'm just a bit put out after a night in the ergot. Harris really should rotate his stock." Jairus dusted himself off. It was a losing battle. "Anyway, I was there yesterday. I'm not going back until the rabble has cleared."

"Rabble?"

"Bikers. Not your normal Harley Davidson orthodontist crowd either. These two were of tougher stock. I don't think either one of them said two words to Dame Williams. I'm not going back until they leave."

"Hmmm. I may have to pay the Nap 'N' Breakkers a visit. Are they still there, do you think?"

"Don't know. Don't care," Jairus said picking up his pack. "I just know I'm going to see if I can make it to West Watershed by 3:00. The Lion's Club is serving an all-day breakfast today."

With that, Dr. Jairus Dishome walked on. Rhapsode walked beside him trying not to look too contrite.

Scott Dobbs was a born drunk, or at least a born drinker. It wasn't that he was drunk all the time. In fact, it could be said that no one in all of Clements had actually seen Scott drunk at any of the backyard get-togethers, wedding dances, or keg parties Scott supposedly attended. Regardless of the occasion, Scott would materialize, beer in hand. Invited or not, he was always welcomed, if rarely noticed.

Scott had spent the last half-hour sitting at the far end of the bar at Lucky's, listening to the guys at the pool table talk. They bragged about girls, trucks, and past drinking binges - some of which Scott actually witnessed firsthand. He had his back to the players, part of his talent for not being seen, when he heard the group go quiet. Then he heard a ball drop.

"There," said Bill Ullage. "You owe me twenty bucks, and another beer."

There was just silence. To Scott, it was like the rattling of a snakes tail. There was no way he was turning around now.

"What?" Bill asked.

"Um, Bill," a quiet voice said. It was probably one of the Simon boys, but Scott wasn't sure. "You didn't call the shot."

"So?"

"Well, you have to call the eight ball. Otherwise the shot doesn't count."

"' the fuck you mean?"

"It doesn't count," said another voice. "It means you sunk the eight ball out of turn. That means you lost."

The jukebox was now playing something off the Cowboy Junkies' 'Trinity' album. Margot Timmins wailed softly through the silence of the bar.

This was the point Scott hated. He knew something was going to happen. Had this been a graduation party he'd been "invited to", he would have quietly snuck out before things got worse. If he moved now, he'd likely become the target. So he sat and disappeared. David Copperfield would have been envious.

"Lost? You think I lost?" Bill wasn't yelling. He was just increasing the tension by pretending he was calm.

"Well..." started someone.

"Just where the fuck else did you think I was going to go with that shot? It went right where I aimed. Dead in. I didn't have to call it. Hell, Stevie Fuckin' Wonder wouldn't have had to call that shot."

"But it was a long bank shot," one of the Simon boys said. "It was across the table. I figured you were going to pocket it in the corner."

It is amazing how well you can hear deep nostril breathing over a quiet song. Scott contemplated just how he would vault the bar. He just wasn't sure he could keep his foot from getting tangled in the fishnet Ralph had tacked to the wall for decoration.

"Well, fuck," Bill eventually said.

There was the sound of a stick being dropped on the felt. Then it started. Scott wasn't moving. Not now. It felt as if there was a sniper in the woods, or a T-Rex. Moving would have been counterproductive to his hiding abilities. He concentrated on becoming transparent.

"Hey you. Harley Boy. Where the hell you from?" Bill shouted to the guy at the far end of the bar. Scott ventured to turn around, just a bit, very slowly.

The stranger was taking a drink from his glass, but he rolled his eyes toward Bill. After a long swallow, he set down his glass. Scott heard the stranger breathe what he thought was the same sigh his father used to give when he was about to lay down a harsh punishment. Scott could see Ralph had moved down the bar, nearer to what Ralph liked to call his Crowd Control Policy. The stranger looked straight ahead at the bar mirror and spoke as if he was talking to his own reflection.

"It is said that people do not change. They cannot. Human nature is ingrained in most, imbedded in some, and imbibed in a sad few." At this last, he turned toward Bill,

"What?" Bill asked.

"Look," the biker said. "I know how these things go. You're pissed off because you lost your girlfriend, your boyfriend, or your pool game. Maybe you lost all three. Regardless of the reason, you are looking to beat the hell out of someone. Obviously, you aren't blaming your friends. They are probably the only friends you've got.

"This guy," Scott froze. The stranger was looking at him. It was a very bad development. "He'd probably melt and let you beat the hell out of him just for breathing. It wouldn't be a challenge."

Scott scanned for all available escape routes. He considered the merits of rolling over the bar and curling into a fetal position.

"So you decided to pick on a stranger," Chord stared directly into Bill's eyes. "I'm the only stranger here, so naturally you want to fight me. How am I doing?"

Bill was starting to fume. Confusion did that to him. "Hey, fuckhead. I asked you where you are from."

"I'm from a place where we don't end our sentences in prepositions."

"What?"

The stranger sighed. "Never mind," he said getting off his barstool. "It's an old joke." He gestured toward the door. "Shall we dance?"

They left the bar together. Two other pool players followed them out.

The last notes of a Mary Osborne tune faded from the jukebox.

"Ralph," Scott said. "I think you are going to need a new pool cue."

Ralph moved his hand away from under the bar and picked up glass number one again. He started to give it its twelfth polish of the day.

"Why do you say that, Scott?"

"I just saw Cecil Simon walk out the back with one."

Ten minutes later, Chord walked back into the bar having put Bill in his place. No one followed him in. His face was scratched, dusty, and a little bit bloody on one side. The other side looked like someone had pressed a Russian branding iron to it. Scott saw what looked like the word "rallipr" on the side of his face. The 'r's were backward, so he assumed it was Russian.

Ralph handed Chord a wet washrag.

"Thanks," the biker said wiping his face and wincing a bit before pressing it to the back of his neck.

"So," Ralph said. "Am I going to have to clean up a mess outside?"

"No, I don't think so. The big guy should get up in a little while."

"You didn't kill him?"

"Nope. It's against my nature. I don't even kill spiders."

"You believe in karma, then?"

"Something like that." Chord sat down. "Hey! My beer's still cold."

The backdoor banged shut. Ralph and Chord both looked up. They were alone in the bar.

"Who just went out?" Chord asked.

"Someone going to get my pool cue I hope."

CHAPTER 3

THE OLD CHEVY NOVA wasn't taking corners well. This might have had to do with the car's oversized tires, or the fact that it had seen better days since it rolled off the factory floor in 1971. It could have been the fact that the driver, Monty Stope, had other things on his mind, such as the wash of small rubber balls and broken glass he could hear rolling and bouncing around the trunk of the car. He tried to steer carefully and not make them slosh so much.

What was really getting to him was that Jed Bushman hadn't said a word to him since they left the Culla Cantina in Deerburg. The big man just sat there pretending to read the paper under the dome light.

"So," Monty ventured. "The taquitos were good."

Jed kept looking at his paper.

"I had the chicken. You had the beef ones, right?"

Still nothing.

"I'm pretty sure that's what you had. I took a quick bite out of one of yours when you got up to pee."

"Hmm." Jed turned a page.

The Nova hit a pothole, shaking the trunk like a giant green maraca. Monty winced. Jed seemed not to hear a thing.

The road twisted through the oak and pine-covered hills. Though the night was overcast and dark, it would have been a pleasant drive. The twists and turns of the highway brought different shapes into focus. The bright red sparkle of mailbox reflectors; the shiny bridge markers over dark creeks; the shadow of a deer bounding off the road into the ditch; all of these materialized in the sweep of the Nova's dusty beams. The headlights did nothing, however, to cut the silence.

"Anything interesting in there?" Monty ventured.

Jed said nothing.

It wasn't that Jed didn't like Monty. Jed had pulled him out of more scrapes than he could count. Most of them weren't his fault exactly, but Monty always felt guilty. There was the time when Jed had to jump off the fishing boat into Lake Michigan. Monty had fallen in trying to grab a stack of twenties that fell out of the transport bag. After that, Jed wasn't in the mood to fish from their "getaway ship."

Then there was the time Jed had to cut the back of Monty's coat. It caught on a door handle on their way into the Quickie Bank in Holister. They were wearing masks. Monty's was an oversized one from a horror movie he pretended he liked, but it was too big for the task. He never saw the door handle. After Jed freed him they just turned around and left.

Now Jed was giving him the silent treatment, all because of some stupid SuperBalls.

The Nova rounded the corner leading onto Peach Pit Road. They only had ten more miles to go.

John Montét

He had to get Jed talking before they got there or he'd really get it from the Dragon Lady - a name he would never call her to her face.

"At least the counter girl was cute."

Jed stared over the top of the paper for a moment and then crumpled it to his lap.

"You really don't get it, do you?" he said.

"Yes I do. I get it."

"No, you don't."

"I do!"

Jed tilted his head to look at Monty for the first time in an hour. "So then, where did you go wrong?"

Monty thought for a moment. He hated these tests. "I didn't get the money."

"No," Jed's patiently instructive tone made Monty even more nervous. "I mean, yes. That was bad, but it wasn't where you went wrong."

Monty thought about it for a moment. He wasn't dumb. He was just a little lost in his own world sometimes.

People often thought he was the smarter of the two. This was largely due to Monty's smaller stature. Jed was six-foot-two and over 250 pounds of muscle. Monty was at least three inches shorter and eighty pounds lighter than Jed.

Monty had something Jed didn't, however. Monty was, in the words of his own grandmother, off his rocker. He wasn't crazy all the time, mind you, but in stressful situations there wasn't anything Monty wouldn't do. He figured it was why Jed was mad at him right now.

"Was it when I ordered the chicken?"

"No! It wasn't when you ordered the

goddamned chicken!"

"Don't swear at me."

"Sorry." Jed tried to control himself. "Think. At what point did the whole thing go wrong?"

Monty swerved a bit to avoid a shiny-eyed raccoon. The trunk rattled.

"It was the SuperBalls, wasn't it?" he said.

"You're getting closer, Monty. What about the SuperBalls went wrong?"

"Was it when I shot the machine?"

"Bingo! Now why was that bad?"

"It wasn't bad. That machine took my quarters. I hate it when machines take your quarters. Stupid machines."

"Whoa, there. I know you didn't like the machine taking your quarters, but why was shooting the machine bad?"

Monty thought again. He remembered how Jed always told him before a job not to get physical with anyone.

"I don't know, Jed. It wasn't like I could have hurt anyone. They were just BB guns."

Jed held the crumpled papers tighter in his enthusiasm. "Exactly! They were just BB guns, Monty - fully automatic BB guns. But until you shot that SuperBall machine, the girl behind the counter didn't know that, did she?"

"No."

"So?"

"So, that's why she tripped the alarm."

"Right. That's why she tripped the alarm and we had to leave."

"Without the money."

Jed made a smacking sound with his lips. "Without the money."

"At least I got most of the SuperBalls, and most of the machine too."

They passed a farmer on a tractor going the opposite direction. Though they couldn't see one another through the spotlights and the darkness, all three waved.

"Think she'll be pissed?" Monty asked.

Jed smoothed out his paper. "Yep."

Church isn't the usual place for the lead singer of an almost all-girl punk rock/techno band, but that was where Tiffany Leitzow found herself on an early Saturday afternoon. She wasn't exactly the religious type. She'd been to church plenty of times. She was even once confirmed in a ceremony so heinous she preferred to think of it as a parentally induced psychotic episode. She did like the naked dude pinned to the front wall, and she considered herself an expert on candles and incense, yet that wasn't enough to keep her from ducking every Sunday since she was fourteen. She wouldn't be there on that particular day but Tiffany needed guidance.

Not from the preacher, mind you. God no. That douche couldn't comprehend the depths of her angst. He'd take one look at her, probably stare at her tits, and then decide she needed to pray until her knees hurt and her jaw ached. Men all thought that way, didn't they?

She could have gone to the cops with her problems, but that wouldn't have done any good. They were all out looking for drunk teenagers and out-of-state license plates so they could fill their widows and orphans funds with their ill-gotten fines. They wouldn't care about her problems. If they did, they would probably lock her up. They might do it just to keep her quiet. Hell, they were probably getting some kickback from Virgil Ferris anyway.

She knelt on the little padded bench behind the pew and tried to remember how to pray. The kneeling bench was the thing she liked best about the Lutheran services, not that she would ever admit it. It was nice to keep changing position during the service. The Lutherans and Catholics all knew that if you keep people moving, they stay interested.

The same was true for music. All the members of Emetic Kitten knew that if you can get people dancing, you could probably play "Sweet Jane" on a 3-foot rubber dong and it wouldn't matter. Trouble was, no one danced at their shows. People just didn't get the deeper connotations of her angst. One day Emetic Kitten would take off. They just needed a better PA. They also needed to play somewhere larger than a garage - preferably with an audience. That would be sweet.

"Tiffany?"

She'd been deep in thought (she was actually silently reciting the words to "Time of Your Life" by Green Day), when Pastor Jessessky snuck up on her. He was standing at the far end of the pew with an odd look on his face, like he'd never seen pink and aqua striped socks with black capris before.

"Hi Pastor John. I was, um, just thinking."

"Normally I wouldn't have interrupted someone at prayer, but you were slowly shaking your head from side to side. I thought you might have been having an episode."

She blushed a bit. "I don't get those anymore. Doctor said it was an allergic reaction to something I ate. They stopped when I quit eating Nutter Butters."

"Oh," he said.

He had nice hair, she noticed. He didn't look half bad for an old guy. He had to be like thirty or something.

"So, we haven't seen you at regular service for a while. How is your family?"

"They go to service every week, Pastor. Don't you know how they are?"

He looked down at the floor for a moment and smiled before lifting his deep blue eyes back to hers.

"Well, certainly," he said. "They seem well, but I'm interested in how you are getting on with them."

"I'm not speaking to Mom, and Dad ignores me completely when football is on. It sucks."

The truth was that she got along great with her mother. The only reason the two of them didn't was because her mother was deaf and had recently scalded both hands while making spaghetti. It was like all her mom could do now was mumble. It would be better when the bandages came off next week. As for her father, no one ever makes small talk when the Packers game is on at the Leitzow house. It was Tiffany who made that rule.

"I can only imagine," the pastor said. "How are your mother's hands these days?"

"Fine, I guess. The bandages come off in a few days."

"And how are the Packers doing?"

"If we could find a decent blocking line, we'd make the playoffs this time."

It was evident that the guy was looking right through her, which she was used to. He wasn't, however, passing judgment and that made her nervous. "I see they took down that creepy abortion billboard in the churchyard."

Pastor John Jessessky seemed willing to let the conversation come his way for a while.

"Yes," he said. "It will be less money spent out of the coffers every month."

"And it was creepy," Tiffany said.

"And it was creepy."

"Gave me the willies."

"You made that point."

Tiffany seemed to dig deep in her pockets for something else to mention. It wasn't easy talking to a squishy celibate man. Pastors were celibate, weren't they? At least he was better than the last Pastor of Our Church of the Virgin. Everything there seemed a little better. Before Pastor Jessessky came, back when old man Williams held congregation, the church's formal name included "elusive" in the title.

"I saw the new plaque on the front door."

"They put it up last month." It wasn't an accusation, but it still made Tiffany blush a bit at her infrequent attendance. Catching her flush, he said, "They did let me move the old statuary."

"Oh. Yeah. I was going to mention that." Even following his gaze, Tiffany had a hard time spotting it. The pastor had yet to convince the church elders to remove the three-foot high stone statue from the altar entirely. To the casual observer, it appeared to be an effigy of a pistol and bottle of whiskey. The elders claimed it was really a Jerusalem turnip and a two-legged lamb, but that was wishful thinking according to Pastor John. Even if one could except that turnips grew square and had nearly decipherable labels, you couldn't get past the inscription "In cuius locum ipse fecissem". "In His place, I would have done the same." It was remarkable that he had managed to convince the elders to let him put it more or less out of sight behind the left-hand chancel. Tiffany could just make it out it in the dim corner light.

It seemed like a good time to leave, but the Pastor blocked her way. Well, he didn't block it. She could have skirted around him, but it would have felt like she was running or just being rude. It was a long way to the other end of the pew. Instead she just sat and fidgeted.

Pastor John looked back at her. "Are you sure you don't want to talk. I listen well."

Dammit. If she didn't tell him something, he would end up talking to her parents, then they would hold one of their little 'talks.' That wouldn't be so bad, but the subject of thousands of missing dolloars would be a tougher topic than that romance novel they caught her reading in fifth grade. It would be better to expel the rest of her conscience to the pastor.

Tiffany stood up and straightened her black and chartruse babydoll tee shirt before launching into her story.

"Okay, so Mom wouldn't even listen to me the other day," she began. "I came home - well, it was a little late - but it wasn't as if she really missed me. I mean, she was going to watch that third episode of that BBC series on PBS, and there were still three episodes to go, not that I watch it, so I didn't think she would mind if I slipped out and went to Debbie's house - she's our drummer - and ran some lyrics by her. She and I are working on a song about that old series, *Buffy the Vampire Slayer*, only our song is about how male vampires have an allergy to wearing shirts, like it is garlic or something, which we think would make a better show anyway. So when I came in - not that much after midnight - she wasn't even watching her show. It was like she didn't even care about getting her daily culture fix and would rather give me the third-degree. She really could use more culture. Have you seen what she's been reading lately? Nothing but quilting books and novels by someone named 'Anais'. It's not that she could hold a book now anyway. You'd think she'd had enough of the second-degree already. You know she really can yell - well, stare - louder than anyone in history. I just said 'whatever, you'll never understand me.' Sure, she couldn't hear me, but I stomped off to bed hard enough that I knew she could feel it. She didn't sign a word - not one - and I don't think the bandages are a decent excuse."

Pastor John simply stared at her as if she was speaking in braille.

"Then I found ten dollars."

He snapped out of his haze. "Pardon?" he asked.

"Never mind." Tiffany found that the only way

to give a point to a pointless story is to add 'and then I found ten dollars.' In this case, that didn't even work.

"I was really just taking a break, Pastor. I should get going."

"Certainly," said Pastor John, still a bit flumuxed by the diatribe. He stepped back to let Tiffany out of the aisle. "I hope to see you again one of these Sunday mornings."

"You never know," Tiffany said trying to avoid looking directly into his baby-blues. "I might."

"Until then, I hope your prayers are answered."

"Sure. Time of my life. See you," she said turning and heading for the door a bit miffed. You'd think even a man of the cloth would have the decency to look at your tits once in a while.

As she stepped outside, she heard a crash. It wasn't loud, but she could hear it over the sound of a truck coming down the hill. It sounded like someone took a big trashcan, slammed it to the ground, then stomped on it a couple of times. Sounded like a heavy trashcan too. She hurried down the wide stone steps to the sidewalk. She looked up the street in time to see two men running away from Lucky's. One she recognized as Cecil Simon. She'd know his ass anywhere. On the ground from where they ran lay a bleeding motorcycle.

CHAPTER 4

LUCKY'S BAR BUZZED with its usual evening business. Several patrons, mostly single men just off work, and a few families wandered in looking for the fried and griddled food Lucky's was famous for - that is if the admiration of a single county constituted fame. The single women wouldn't be in until they had a chance to fix their hair and pair up. That would take several more hours.

Patrons chatted at tables and stood in cordial pools around the bar as the piquant smell of grilling meat filled the air with a light, smoky haze. The air hung with the greasy smell of French fries, onion rings, and previously frozen poppers. A lone figure stood inside Lucky's front window and slathered butter on large Kaiser rolls, dropping them on the grill with a delectable hiss. The figure continued a well-choreographed juggling act of grilling tasks while staring steadfastly out through the hazy glass.

That lone master of the grill wasn't Ralph. Ralph wasn't one to cook. In fact, no one had ever seen him do it. Instead, he hired a never-ending string of college-age kids to do the work for him. While there seemed to be someone new cooking each month, the food was always good and never seemed to vary in presentation or taste. Ralph always claimed the flavor was in the grill. He also said it was because he held back a pint of grease when he cleaned out the fryer wells every other month - well, every few months anyway.

Chord wasn't watching the grill, or looking out of the window. Instead, he watched the people come into the noisy bar from his stool. He'd washed his face staunched the bleeding. His headache still pounded in the back of his skull, but it was slowing its tempo to more of a waltz than a tango. He looked down at the half-eaten burger that lay in front of him. It had tasted very good, but odd, like it wasn't really cow. It might have been bison. The cheese was definitely Havarti. The thin slice of grilled Bermuda onion put the initial bite over the top. He would have gladly finished it, but he just couldn't stomach the whole thing with the pounding in his head.

He might have a concussion. Hell, in that condition, he shouldn't even get on a bike. Not that he had a choice. He had to get to Waterloo in another six hours. Then he'd be able to make the delivery, sleep a little, and get something else to eat. Thinking about it though, it would be difficult to find a burger this good, late at night in Waterloo. Cedar Falls might have something. Cradling the slightly crispy bun in his hands, he turned his attention back to the burger.

Dave Matthews was singing about not drinking the water when someone came in and interrupted Chord in mid bite. "Mister. That your bike out front?"

It took a good thirty seconds to finish chewing and swallowing the bite of (elk?) burger before

Chord could answer. The man, dressed as a retired farmer in cowboy boots, flannel shirt, and spotless seed corn cap waited patiently for Chord to finish.

"Probably," Chord smacked. "Where was it?"

"Supine," the man said.

"Beg pardon?"

"Sorry. I'm in chiropractic. It's lying on its side."

"What?" Chord exclaimed as he dropped the burger to the plate and rushed outside.

His bike lay prostrate in the road. Someone had pushed it over, hard. Gas poured from the tank and snaked its way toward the curb as if the bike had sustained an arterial head wound.

"Fuck!" Chord exclaimed. "Fuck, fuck, fuck, fuck, fuck. Fuck!"

He happened to catch a mother and father looking at him oddly as they lead their five year-old son into Lucky's. "Bummer," he heard the boy say.

Ralph was standing beside him now, a mug of steaming highland grog in his hand. "Looks like it was tipped over, stabbed, and leapt upon."

Chord couldn't speak. He couldn't even move to pick up the bike. Wide-eyed fury glued him to the spot. His hands clenched white as he stared at the bike, a burning hate welling up inside him.

There is a rage, unknown by the civilians who drive the highways on four wheels. This rage is reserved for those who do the unspeakable. You can insult a biker. You can call his mother names and claim he has an illegitimate father. In many circumstances, you can even punch a biker and he'll laugh it off. But not even Peter Fonda himself has leave to touch a biker's ride. Going so far as to vandalize a bike will often result in that rarest of opportunities - the chance to hold your own bare trachea in your hand.

"Judging by the size of that dent," Ralph said pointing with his mug. "I'd say that it was done with some fairly big boots. Wouldn't you?"

"Boots?" Chord's teeth would probably never unclench again.

"Big ones. Maybe work boots."

Chord took a deep breath to stop tensing for a moment. It was cutting off blood flow to his brain. The headache had ramped up to a mambo. Still, Ralph was making sense. "So you think," he finally said. "Maybe about a size fourteen."

Ralph took a sip of his coffee. "About that, I'd say."

Chord gave it some time to sink in. Here he was, in a small Iowa town, just a few hours from his delivery destination. His baby - his bike - was fucked up and unrideable. All he really had was his motorcycle. Hell, his pack held most of his worldly possessions. It was still tied to the bike, touching the ground and soaking up gas as he stood there and thought. He'd have to get moving somehow. He had a delivery to make.

Then there was the matter of Bill Ungulate, or whatever the hell Ralph said his name was. Part of him, a very big part, wanted to find the son of a bitch and tear him into tiny unidentifiable pieces. That would take time, however. It would also draw far too much attention to him and his situation. It is amazing how refraining from just one good head stomp can come back to haunt you.

"I'm going to have to get this thing fixed, Ralph."

"So I see."

"You got a good bike shop here in town?"

"No. There is one up in Colubra, but that's a good fifty miles away. You won't get Jefferies to tow you that far tonight."

"What are my options then?"

"Well, were it me, I would talk to Neil."

"Neil?"

"Neil Clark. He knows everyone in the area. He used to be into motorcycles if I remember. I'm guessing he knows a guy who could help you. You have to talk to him anyway."

"I do?"

"Of course," Ralph said as if this was the simplest fact in the world.

Chord squeezed his eyes shut hard, trying to restart his thought process; then he opened them again and looked back to Ralph. "How do I get hold of Neil Clark? Is his number in the book?"

"Yeah, but you don't have to bother calling him. He's coming now." Ralph pointed up the street. Red and blue lights danced off the brick walls of the buildings as the cruiser approached the bar.

"What you're saying is that Neil Clark is-"

"Officer Neil Clark - our county sheriff. Voted for him myself, twice."

"Well," Chord said, trying hard to suppress the sudden urge to sprint in the opposite direction. "Isn't that convenient?"

John Montét

Dogs are always positive about two things - squirrels and sausage. Rhapsode was in a quandary over the former. There was obviously a squirrel in the tree under which Jairus napped, happily digesting. The problem was that the squirrel wasn't making any noise. It was just laying up there, maybe in a nest. Maybe it found a hole. Squirrels like holes. He couldn't actually see it, but he could certainly smell it.

Not that Rhapsode was hungry. He'd had his fill of sausage, pancakes, and orange juice at the West Watershed Lions Club. He liked it there. It wasn't just the food. The humans there let him come into the building. Jairus had long ago convinced them that he was a service dog, though Rhapsode only knew one trick. He could catch pieces of breakfast sausage before they hit the ground. He never missed. Sometimes, when people weren't actually looking, he'd do the trick before anyone even thought of throwing the sausage. A plate is a dumb place to put sausage anyway.

Actually, the problem with this squirrel was two-fold. First, it was up there. Dogs don't actually climb trees (which is why we still have squirrels); so it wasn't possible for Rhapsode to get a first-hand taste... er, look at the squirrel. The second problem was the smell. It smelled odd. It was as if it had gotten into some sort of perfume. It wasn't a good smell. Rhapsode didn't like perfume. It reminded him of the woman back at the Humane Society. She was nice enough, but always locked him in a cage at night. She also talked baby talk to him. Rhapsode loathed baby talk.

The squirrel was lying in an owl's nest in a hollow near the top of the tree in a sickening, sweet haze of Tommy Boy - the scent of choice of choosy strippers everywhere. The hole was an old nest full of feathers, twigs, and owlet dung. The squirrel was hoping the smell of the perfume would give way to the smell of owlet so he could once again try to court the red doe squirrel he'd been after since the beginning of the season. Sure, the mating season was over, but why should that stop true love?

It wasn't working, though. His last hope was that the beetles who had taken up residence in the nest would clean him off, or at least cover him with beetle scent. However, they had all scampered away soon after he lay down in the detritus of the nest. He tried to be as still and quiet as he could and hope they would come back. Tommy Boy, as it turned out, was a very effective beetle repellent.

The squirrel was completely aware of the dog at the base of the tree. Even with the Ode du Skankette causing his nose to run, he could tell there was a far-too-interested canine at the base of the tree. It just made things that much more nerve-wracking for a rodent. His encounter with the old woman had been bad enough.

Just two miles away, the red doe squirrel was having her own encounter. She'd followed the scent of peanuts for a couple of tree miles. She'd smelled and eaten peanuts before in the birdfeeders some people kept. They were great, but this smell was intoxicating. It didn't help that it mingled with the reasonably fresh scent of a certain buck squirrel she had seen flitting about the upper branches of the nearby trees. He hadn't made a move yet - he had just tried to show off his climbing and leaping and tail twitching - but anything could happen. Off-season mating was just fine as long as the rest of the scurry didn't find out. A doe had to watch her reputation.

Then she found the peanut. It was huge, though a little flat. It was easily longer than her back leg. It was flat on both sides and it had a sweet, creamy center. Even the shell was soft and delicious!

It wasn't until she was half done eating it that she thought to look for the buck. Popping up on her hind legs, she swiveled around. She was in a cage! Frantically, she scampered in all twelve directions, but there was no way out. Two of the walls were slanted. One was the way she came in. She tried to get under the wall, to push the slant up, but it didn't work.

The doe began to panic. She screeched and chattered, running around the tiny cage in a flurry of noise and fear. She was so desperate she didn't see or smell the old lady coming.

"Now, now, my smelly little sciurine friend," she said with what could only be described as a slight cackle. "We'll see if we can get you nice and pretty again. You smell something awful."

The old lady picked up the cage and started walking home, the doe alternating between frozen fear and hysterical panic. The woman didn't bother picking up the last half of the Nutter Butter cookie that fell through the cage to the ground.

◆ ◇ ☠ ◇ ◆

In the dark, quiet driveway of the Nap 'N' Breakkers bed and breakfast, the engine of a monstrous motorcycle quietly pinged as it cooled. A daisy was painted carefully on the side of the black and chrome machine's gas tank. Beside the motorcycle, real daisies and multi-colored petunias stood at attention along the driveway, poking from the woodchip edging that ran down both sides of the asphalt. Tall decretive grasses poked up here and there - a sharp contrast to the lush, green grass of the lawn. It gave the two-story, five-bedroom home an inviting feeling. There were no garden gnomes, plywood silhouettes of people bending over, or spinning pin-wheeled roadrunners to be found. A pink flamingo wouldn't have lasted two seconds - not in June William's lawn. Those things were for the tacky masses that didn't have the wherewithal to do even the most cursory study of landscape design. It's called a "library", people. Taste can be read into a brain.

June looked out of the second story window at all three of the bikes in the driveway. None of them were Harley Davidsons. It was too bad. While she didn't ride, June made a point of knowing bikes and their worth. Harleys meant disposable income. When the riders normally stop in Clements, often on their way to Anamosa from the Cities or on their way to Algona from Wisconsin, she could up the boarding prices by 20 percent and they never batted an eye. What was it Kenneth called them, Rich Urban Bikers

- "Rubbers", was it?

Not that June Williams normally needed money. She usually had plenty. The last governor had been a big fan of her brand of services. It wasn't her overnight accommodations of course. Each governor had the run of the historical mansion at the top of the hill whenever they stayed in the county. It was a perk of the office. What the last governor had enjoyed was the soundproofed, dungeon-style playroom in the upper floor of the Nap 'N' Breakkers. It was so odd how the powerful eroticized the loss of power and the handing over of control.

June enjoyed the visits as well. She knew she looked good wearing thigh-high stiletto boots, a crotchless half-cup corset and nipple rouge. Her long dark brown hair, yoga toned body, and alabaster skin made her flat-out intimidating. She could also swing a whip with the best of them, hitting the end of a penis at ten feet and not leave more than a little red mark and a lasting mental impression.

Ten years of for-hire sexual domination, and two separate government clients, had set her up with a nest egg the size of a small city budget. Had she not invested in the stock market so heavily, she would still be sitting pretty. As it stood, she didn't have nearly enough to make the move to Seattle where should could open her own underground house of domination. She couldn't be Mistress for much longer before age and gravity made her pick up the reigns as Madame.

What she needed now was a fair amount of extra cash. It had to come soon and as quietly as possible. Thanks to this particular group of bikers, she could manage that very thing - if she played it just right. What she'd heard them discuss on the porch earlier had been a pleasant surprise.

Soon after their arrival, she'd showed them where they would be sleeping and the guest refrigerator. She had explained that the cost of what was used in the fridge would be split among the bills, but to help themselves to all the frozen pizza and beer they'd like. The Coors they'd have to buy on their own. June, like Ralph, refused to stock industrial beer.

After settling her guests in for the evening, June retired, heading up to her room on the top floor at the front of the house. She was standing at the window, contemplating the mental impact of ostrich boots worn over black leather pants when she caught the conversation on the porch.

"I'm telling you that's how they move them. They give them to bikers and have them do the transport." It sounded like the guy who came in on a rather custom looking Buell motorcycle.

"But why not hire an armored car? Then at least you'd have armed escort." It was the older gentleman who rode the restored Moto Guzzi.

"Sure," said Buell. "But just think how conspicuous that is. Plus there is a paper trail a mile wide. If they get caught, the feds can trace it back without breaking a sweat. I don't care how good they are."

The woman who came in on the huge Triumph spoke up. She'd arrived later, but looked just as frayed around the edges. They had all ridden some distance it seemed.

"It also makes sense from the standpoint of the competition. Just think how many riders come through this area. What, tens of thousands per year? An armored car would stick out like a sore plum."

"Thumb," Buell said.

"I know what I said."

"And you're saying," Moto Guzzi picked up. "That one of these runners is coming through this way?"

"Exactly," Buell said. "Hell, I'm thinking he's either coming through tonight, or maybe tomorrow. I've got a guy checking for me in The Cities. I've cut him in for one percent if this works out."

"One percent," Triumph said. "That's not much of an incentive."

"Yeah, but if I'm right, and the diamonds are on him, my contact stands to clear fifty grand easy."

June leaned out of the window a bit more at the mention of diamonds.

"Wait a minute." Moto Guzzi said. "That would mean the total haul would have to be-"

"Five million!" Triumph girl completed. June's eyebrows made a sudden dash for her hairline.

"Thanks." Moto Guzzi said.

"I'm in," Triumph said.

"Yeah, me too."

"Good!" Buell said. "We'll have a timeline, the courier's route, and a description in the morning. We should be able to pull it off without a hitch. I even have a purchaser lined up. It will be a piece of cake."

June leaned back inside the window. She had a purchaser in mind as well - one that was way up on the black market totem pole. The idea of getting her hands on the diamonds made her palms itch. If she played it right, found their weak spot and exploited it in just the right way, she'd be able to clear enough to set up shop in Seattle.

She slowly closed the window. As she did so, it dislodged a formerly secreted walnut from the corner of the window box. It rolled down the eaves and into the gutter with a soft thunk.

"What was that?" Buell asked.

Triumph leaned out over the porch railing and looked up. The lights in the upstairs windows were off. "Squirrels, I suppose," she said.

"Damn squirrels," said Buell.

"Hey," said Moto Guzzi. "Are either of you wearing perfume?

CHAPTER 5

IT TOOK JUST FIFTEEN MINUTES for Sheriff Clark to call for the tow truck, get the bike loaded, secure it onto Kenneth Jefferies' towing flatbed, and make arrangements for Chord to pick up his belongings later after the gas had some time to evaporate at the shop. Sheriff Clark wouldn't let Chord take his essentials back to the station until the smell and risk of fire died down a bit. In the meantime, they drove the five blocks down the street to the station house to file the paperwork.

The sheriff's office, like every other office along Main Street, was located in a two-story brick building circa 1890. It had the same white trim and short stoop that marked nearly every building along the street. It wasn't from a deep sense of civic pride that the city council maintained Clements's anachronistic appeal. It was that over time they had systematically registered every building along the main drag as a state historic site. It was short cash, but it helped to keep some of the other roads paved, and it funded the annual city board meeting and camping trip to Minnesota.

The inside of the station house presented a dichotomized assortment of sheriff clichés. Aged wood furniture quarreled with sterile office pieces. A framed needlepoint hung next to the seeming overly unattended bulletin board displaying Rhotic County's "Most Wanted". The tall receptionist desk looked like it belonged in a dentist's office. The room smelled of cheap coffee, stale pastries, and something slowly dying in the dorm-sized refrigerator. Two doors took up most of the far wall. Above one, hung a wood burned sign that read "Lockup". Above the other door, directly behind the reception desk, another wood-burned sign read "Sherrif's Office".

"Nice creative spelling," Chord said, glancing up at the sign as Sheriff Clark held the door for him to enter the back office.

"Margret's nephew did the signs in shop class," Clark said. "We didn't have the heart to tell him. Most visitors never even notice."

Chord dropped into the chair to which the sheriff gestured. He tried to look more nonchalant than he felt. He considered propping his feet on the desk, but decided that would have been going too far.

"I'm sorry," he said. "Who's Margret?"

The sheriff tapped the keyboard on the desk with the absent rapidity of someone trying to wake up a computer.

"Margret Strangeland is our dispatcher."

"You have a dispatcher?"

The sheriff continued to stare at the screen as he clicked the mouse a few times and found the home row. "Dispatcher is a higher pay grade than receptionist," he said. "She has been with us for fifteen years."

As the sheriff typed and clicked, Chord looked around at the décor. Two high bookshelves dominated the room. Titles such as "Drug Enforcement in the Modern Age" and "The Criminal Capacity for Deception" stood neatly next to other less legal titles such as "Ulysses", "Modern Religion", and "American Gods". There were the usual framed certificates behind the sheriff's desk, though Chord could only make out a few of them. At least three seemed to be diplomas and one was a citation, but he couldn't tell for what. Absent from the wall décor was the ubiquitous human-shaped target with neat deadly looking bullet holes. Perhaps our sheriff isn't a very good shot, Chord thought.

The window in the wall to the right of the desk looked out through a mass of street-lit vegetation. Trees along the banks of the Mismate River ran along the top of a ten-foot stone embankment just outside the office. Chord figured it must take a rock climber to wash the outside of the windows.

"Mr. Chord," Clark said from behind the desk.

"Michael, please," Chord said turning to sit down again.

"Michael. We need to fill out the incident report. I have most the information entered, but I need your license to complete the process. May I see it?"

Chord pulled his wallet out of the pocket of his jacket and handed it to the sheriff. Though right-handed, Chord kept his wallet in his right inside jacket pocket. This made it possible to keep the left side tight to his body so as not to reveal the gun he kept there. Well, the gun he usually kept there. The gun and holster were rolled up in some gas-soaked underwear in his pack. He wasn't planning on wearing it until the pickup - the gun, that is.

In getting the bike situated on the flatbed, Chord had managed to get a good look at the damage. It wasn't terrible; at least he didn't think it was. It was hard to get a read on the tow truck driver. The man talked in the manic manner of someone who had way too much coffee. That, and his thick Iowa/Minnesota accent made it hard to understand what he was saying. Chord did manage to double-check the front of the frame. It looked to be intact. The drop certainly wouldn't have hurt diamonds tucked away inside.

"Mr. Chord," the sheriff said, interrupting Chords thoughts.

"Yeah?"

"Is all of the information on your license current?"

"Yes."

"You have your address listed as '120 Kellogg Boulevard West' in St Paul. Is that correct?"

"Yes."

"You are sure?"

Chord decided to start on the defensive. "I live there don't I?"

"I wouldn't know," Clark said. "However my best guess is that you don't. That is, unless you happen to be sleeping on the interactive barge."

"What?"

A smirk crept onto the sheriff's face. "Mr. Chord," he began.

"Michael."

"Michael. The address on your license is the

address for the Science Museum of Minnesota. I've been there quite often. I don't remember seeing you."

Until the sheriff started questioning him, Chord had forgotten that he'd pulled a random address out of the phone book to use on his license. A scanner, some document software, and a copy of a power bill were all that was needed to convince the Minnesota Department of Transportation that it was his address. They never checked. Nor had he. The whole thing was just a safeguard in case he was shaken down on a drop. It was a very bad idea to let the kind of company he did business with know your real address. It hadn't occurred to him that a cop would cross-reference the information.

"It must be a typo," Chord said. "That isn't the right number."

"A typo? So you are saying you live on Kellogg next to the museum?"

"No, it isn't a typo. It's... it's a palindrome."

"I beg your pardon?"

Chord knew he'd lost. He'd been beaten up, dined on strange and delicious mystery meat served by a landlocked would-be ship's captain, and had his one and only ride out of this one-hit of a town tipped over and desecrated. Now he was quoting Monty Python in order to win an argument with law enforcement.

"Never mind," Chord said. "No, it isn't correct. I'm essentially homeless. I just needed an address so I could get a cell phone. If it is any consolation, I do stop by the museum from time to time to see if they have any mail for me."

"And?" Clark eyes were smiling now.

"They never have any mail for me."

"Astonishing," Clark said. "Have you a place to stay for the night?"

He hadn't thought about staying the night. This would seriously push things back. That wouldn't be good.

"I thought I would just move on. I'll rent a car and come back in the morning."

The sheriff looked at him with one eyebrow raised. Chord supposed Clark was trying his best not to be intimidating. It wasn't working. Under the officer's gaze, Chord felt as if his junk was hanging out.

"I'm afraid we don't have a rental agency here in town, Mr. Chord. In any regard, I need to hold on to your license for a bit. Driving would be out of the question. I'm sure you understand."

"Sure." Chord drew out the word like a sigh.

The sheriff stood up and walked out from behind his desk. "Am I to assume you have an important appointment?" He didn't wait for an answer. "Where, may I ask? Maybe we can get you a ride from someone here in town. If they happen to be going that way that is."

"Des Moines. I'm supposed to help my aunt move."

"I see," Clark said. "I'll ask around. If I hear of someone going to Des Moines this evening, I'll let you know."

"Thanks," Chord said. The sheriff was standing in front of him. He was almost a full head taller than Chord.

"Why don't you stay here tonight? There is no

one else in the cells. We aren't expecting Otis to walk in until after midnight, so you'll have some time to yourself."

"Otis?" Chord looked at the sheriff. The small smile lines in the corners of Clark's eyes deepened. Clark was fucking with him.

"Got it," Chord said. "Under arrest, am I?"

"Let's call it surveillance. It's less paperwork." Clark put a hand on Chord's shoulder and led him gently out of his office and toward Lockup. "I won't even lock the door. You can come and go as you wish. But don't scare Margret in the morning. You'll get Tased."

"You're that protective of your staff?"

"No, but Margret is a bit jumpy before she has her coffee in the morning. Tread softly until 10:00 AM."

"Thanks for the warning."

Lockup turned out to be two cells facing each other across a short hall. A half-filled water cooler hummed gently between the cells. Chord noticed that it was in easy reach of either cell even if they were locked. He walked into one of the cells and turned around to watch the sheriff leave.

"Hey," he called after him. "How's the cellphone coverage in here."

"Lousy." The sheriff closed the door to Lockup behind him.

"Great," Chord said.

The water cooler just outside the cell bubbled.

Tiffany Leitzow sat on a hillside. She was watching a boat sail gracefully across the man-made lake. She often came to the spot when she needed to think. When Tiffany was in a better mood, she would imagine all the crap that must be at the bottom. With all stoners at the campgrounds on the far end of the lake, there had to be three hundred bongs down there by now. Maybe there was treasure, boxes of cash dropped by fleeing bank robbers. Maybe there was even a body - a mafia hit no one would ever solve because the dead guy was someone no one would ever miss.

In truth, there was no mafia in Clements. There also hadn't been a bank robbery in Rhotic County in fifteen years. In fact, the largest amount ever taken in a bank robbery in the county was $142, and it was all in quarters. Also, as any reputable stoner will tell you - bongs are expensive.

The only odd things at the bottom of the lake were three dozen bowling balls. These had fallen through the ice after the Big Thaw of '98 had taken the Mallard Lake Outdoor Bowling Tournament by surprise - much to the relief of the pinsetters from Scout Troop 6.

That night, Tiffany was as oblivious to the bowling balls as to the line of ants currently hauling sugar from a broken Pixy Stix in her back pocket. In fact, it is doubtful she would notice a sparkling vampire if one happened by. (One never happened by.) It wouldn't matter if one did. She was too upset to do anything but brood. The talk with Pastor Jessessky might have helped if she told him the truth. The busted motorcycle and the sight of Cecil Simon's tush was a nice distraction until the cops showed up. Then her whole shitty situation sank back in. So, as she sat on the hill watching the fading light of the sun sink below the distant bumpy horizon, she tried to decide if she was just dating the pooch or if they'd gone all the way.

Tiffany worked nights at the local Fareway grocery store. She stocked shelves, ran the register, and poked through the frozen foods for expired items. She'd been there long enough to get out of mop duty most of the time. The year before, Mr. Ferris had even started letting her help with the nightly accounts when she worked the late shift. Sure he was kind of a creep; she'd caught him staring at her tits loads of times. But it wasn't like he was any different from any of the other old cougar pervs in town. Besides, he never stood within three feet of her, even when he was teaching her how to use the register.

Tiffany loved math. Even more, she liked to run computer programs that did the math for her. She'd been writing computer code for three years, which is like forever in computer terms. Once Mr. Ferris showed her how to count the tills and run it against the baseline, she was sure she could write a better program. So, she took a crack at it and spent two weeks hammering out computer code at night after her homework was done. Once she nailed it, she saved the program to the flash drive that she always kept on a thin lanyard. The thought of loading it up on the work computer sent the zombie butterflies spinning in her tummy, but she really didn't expect Ferris to ever notice a new program on his computer.

He wasn't exactly a power user. He was using Excel to do the books, for fuck's sake. He couldn't even write a nested "if" formula. It was just redonkulous.

The program worked great, right after she released the 1.02 version (she forgot to convert back to Base 10 the first time around) she installed it on Mr. Ferris' Dell. The problem was that Mr. Ferris didn't realize it wasn't Excel. She thought that making the whole thing look like a spreadsheet would help Mr. Ferris run the program. On the other hand, she'd also hoped that by making the shortcut icon look like a big green "X", Mr. Ferris wouldn't really notice and would somehow like it that much better. It backfired, big time.

Two nights before her current brooding session, Mr. Ferris had called Tiffany into his office. He sounded upset.

"Leitzow," as a former high school basketball coach, he called all of his employees by their last name. "Get in here. I need your help."

Tiffany was in the backside of the cooler searching for Gorton's fish sticks that had expired within the last two weeks.

"Coming," she called.

When she entered the office, Mr. Ferris was craning his neck forward, trying to squint through his tortoiseshell glasses at a screen that wasn't a foot from this nose. "How do I put in past balances? I'm not getting it. You'd think I'd be able to remember."

Tiffany skirted the edge of the desk and looked at the screen and the program he was using. It wasn't Excel. It was Tiffany's program, which she'd dubbed EKKA (Emetic Kitten Kicks Ass, trademark pending).

While it had a passing resemblance to Excel, any jackwagon under 30 could have seen it wasn't. A forty-two year-old codger like Mr. Ferris didn't really have a chance.

Tiffany pointed to the screen. "Well, Mr. Ferris, you just have to put it in that cell there, under 'Past Amounts'. I suppose I, er, they should have called it 'Past Balances'. I bet version 1.03 has it right. I'll see what I can do."

"Thanks, Leitzow. I'm not sure what I thought I was missing. It is like this thing changes every night." He sat up, regaining some of his composure. He still hadn't looked away from the screen.

"That all you need?" She was anxious to get back to something mindless so she could run some new code in her head. That, and she was working on a new song. It was about a psycho killer who always wore a yellow raincoat, smelled like fish, and disposed of his victims in ovens set for 425 degrees.

"Yeah, that's it. You can get back to work Leitzow," he said arching his hands like a pianist about to start a concerto.

Tiffany left.

Two hours later, when Mr. Ferris went to take a leak, Tiffany wandered back into his office. She pulled the lanyard with her flash drive over her head, uncapped it, and stuck it into the front of the computer. Two minutes later, she'd downloaded all of the files she needed to make sure the program worked with the current numbers.

When she finally got to work with the program the next day, making the changes was easy. But, when she ran the data models, and checked the notations, she really started to worry. None of the numbers matched. They were all moving to another account. Worse, the files that stored the transaction information, looked as if someone had been changing things around - a lot.

That was the previous night, however. Looking over Mallard Lake from the hillside, while pleasant in an outdoorsy meditative way, wasn't doing anything to ease Tiffany's mind. She'd stayed up most of the night thanks to Red Bull and plenty of Social Distortion. While she'd managed to crack the data issue, she didn't like it. Either the produce department was selling kohlrabi and jicama at $2,000 a pound, or something was seriously wrong with her code. She had written a SSL transfiguration sub-routine that moved the money into the Fareway business bank account. All Mr. Ferris had to do is be sure to drop off the deposit each night so the numbers matched and he could use the new numbers right away in the morning. Only, the numbers could never match. There was too much going into the account. Unless Mr. Ferris really was depositing an extra five figures each week, she was sunk.

The only decision to make now was what prison tattoo to get first. At least she had some Pixy Stix left.

It wasn't the first time that the help had pissed off June Williams and she doubted it would be the last. However, staring at an open trunk full of

SuperBalls, broken glass, and twisted tin was throwing her off her rhythm. She couldn't work up a good head of steam through her confusion.

"What I don't understand," she started to say to the two men flanking her. She paused a moment before repeating herself. "What I don't understand, is why bring the machine with you? Why did you bother?"

Jed stood with his arms folded, his back to the trunk. "I asked him that too." He just couldn't look at the mess anymore.

June turned to Monty. "Well?"

Monty hadn't taken his eyes off all of the balls since Jed opened the trunk. All the colors and round shapes scattered around the trunk made his head spin. They were just so cool.

"Well," Monty started. "I only hit the top. When we left, I grabbed it figuring there were more balls in it than there was on the ground. The rest of the glass didn't break until we put it in the trunk and started driving. Plus, it does have money in it."

June turned to him, daring him to meet her gaze. "And how much to you suppose is in the machine, Monty?"

"Well," Monty said, "at fifty cents a pop, there has to be a couple hundred in there. That's not too bad, is it?"

"And was the machine full of SuperBalls when you shot it?"

"Yeah."

"Wouldn't that mean that very few balls had been sold?"

Monty's mind worked fast when it did work. He

immediately saw the problem. "Yeah. That means there isn't much money in there, I guess."

"There's at least fifty cents," Jed said.

"And what do you suppose we do now, gentlemen? What would be your next move of criminal genius?"

"We break the thing open and get out what we can. At least we can do that," Monty said.

"And then?" she asked.

Jed and Monty both stood for a moment before Monty said "There's an Applebee's in Deerburg..."

June slammed the trunk.

"Forget Applebee's," she said, walking back toward the Morton building at the back of the property. Monty and Jed followed. "I have something else for you to do, something that doesn't involve vending machines, SuperBalls, or either of you getting in the way of trouble, at least not directly."

"We're on it, Boss," Monty said. The others stopped walking to look at him. "Whatever it is," he amended.

June opened the door on the Morton building. "What do you two know about transporting diamonds?"

Monty and Jed looked at each other.

June was already inside.

CHAPTER 6

THE CELLPHONE COVERAGE in the holding cell was indeed terrible. It took three tries and two dropped calls before Chord finally figured out it was the bars of the cell causing the issue. He wandered out of the cell and tested the Lockup door. As Clark promised, it was unlocked. Beyond, the reception area was empty. He could see through the small teller window into the office that the sheriff hadn't returned. He was a trusting soul, our sheriff. Well, not so trusting. The door to his office was locked. Chord thought about trying all of the filing cabinets and the drawers of the reception desk, just to see how trusting these folks were but it didn't seem worth the energy.

He flopped hard onto the vinyl couch and checked his phone; full bars. Good, he thought, and dialed his contact's number. It picked up on second ring.

"What the flippin' heck do you want you gal dang donkey bottom?" barked the phone.

"Jeez, a little hostile Jack?"

"Chord?" Jack said. "You're the one that keeps calling me and hanging up? Aren't I going to see you in, what, three hours?"

"Yeah, sorry about the calls. The cell bars were interfering with reception. It kept dropping the call."

"The bars don't do it Mike. They just indicate how good a signal you have. Don't you know how to work a cell phone?"

"No, not the bars on my cell phone, Jack. I mean the bars of the jail cell."

Shit. Wait for it, he thought.

There was a long pause on the other end. Chord knew it was Jack just gathering steam. He could almost hear him vibrating. Jack Dockage was a very nervous man. He'd raised five kids, all of them girls. Being a staunch Catholic, the two things he couldn't stand were the thought of one of his daughters kissing a boy, and cussing. The fact that his youngest daughter was now in her second year of marriage helped his nervousness only a bit. He still had trouble swearing.

"Prison? You irresponsible ne'er-do-well! How the flippin', mother-loving heck did you land your sorry bottom into prison? What did you do, hold up a spirits establishment? It's bad enough that I stuck my neck out on this deal. I can't believe you'd have the ever-loving audacity to chop off my private bits like this. It takes a special kind of sinner, one with really huge gonads, to get himself arrested on a run like this. If you don't get your-"

"Wait. Did you just say 'gonads', Jack?"

Jack paused, but Chord could still hear him breathing heavily on the other end. "Yeah. I said 'gonads'. I'm sorry, I'm just really peeved off right now."

"I guess. You never use language like that.

Anyway, I'm not arrested."

"But you're in prison. You're under suspicion of something, I take it."

"The sheriff called it surveillance. He's a little put off that my driver's license says I live at the Minnesota Museum of Science."

"Why would it say that?"

"Random chance. It wasn't intentional."

"For that, he arrested you?"

"No, he didn't arrest me. I'm just at the station for the night. I can come and go if I want. I just can't get anywhere until morning."

Jack took his time processing the information. Thirty seconds later he stopped. "Nope. Don't get it. If you're not arrested, and you can come and go as you please, why are you not calling me from the road on your way down here?"

There was another storm of near swearing on the horizon, Chord could tell.

"Well," he began, "For two reasons. First, talking on a cellphone while driving is a bad idea. To do it while riding a motorcycle is insane."

"You could have pulled over." Jack loved hypotheticals.

"Yes, but that would mean I had a working bike to ride. As of an hour or so ago, I don't."

"What do you mean? You weren't gambling were you?"

"What? No. Somebody, I have an idea who, vandalized my bike. The cargo is safe, but there is a serious hole in the gas tank, some denting, tons of scratches, and God knows what else. I won't have a full report until the mechanic gets done looking at it in another hour or so. It isn't going to be rideable for at least a day, that much is certain."

As Chord knew it would, the next storm came. Jack let loose a rampage of near swearing and anatomically correct terms that would make a kindergartener think twice before repeating. Chord just let it play out. Chord once witnessed Jack fly into a ten-minute bender just because someone dared to suggest that Pope wore silk panties. It wasn't a pretty scene, though the elderly ladies in the checkout line at the Megamart seemed to enjoy the show.

After five minutes, Jack calmed down enough to say "Okay. I'm calmed down. What is the soonest you can get here?"

"That depends," Chord said. "When can you get here?"

"Where, exactly, is 'here'?"

"Clements."

"Clements? Isn't that up on 324 somewhere?"

"Yeah. Only here they call it Main Street."

"Of course they do. That's what, less than two hours away? I can do that. Only, I can't leave for little while. I'm expecting a call. Give me six hours and I'll be there. That will give you time to grab your stuff."

"Thanks, Jack. I'll be at the station house."

"Oh no you won't. I'm not going anywhere near the cop shop. Meet me somewhere else."

"I didn't know you had such a thing against law enforcement. Okay. I'll be at a place called Lucky's. It's on the main drag."

"Lucky's. Got it. Be there." Jack hung up.

Chord put the phone down and laid his head back. He'd have to get things moving soon. All he needed was a little nap before checking in with Jefferies to see how his bike was doing. He was trying to think of a way to get the mechanic away from the bike long enough to get at the stash in the frame when he fell fast asleep.

The phone rang in a quiet housing development in Naperville, Illinois. A professor in political science, Jeet Kune Do expert, and NRA High Master reached the phone from a dead sleep before it rang twice.

"Yes?" he said.

"It's J.D.," said the phone.

"Yes?"

"New job."

"Details?"

"Clements, Off 324. A place called Lucky's. Six hours."

"Target?"

"Code Three Note. Absconding with delivery."

"Three Note?"

"Frickin' yes, Three Note. Jiminy Christmas!"

"Calm yourself. Volume?"

"Doesn't matter. Collateral doesn't matter either."

"Range?"

"Standard pay, plus double expenses. I need the package, though."

"Done."

"Good. I-"

The phone hit the cradle with exactitude.

Kenneth Jefferies ran a clean shop, but it gave the air of being a collection of automotive junk. You wouldn't know it by looking around, but that was perfectly intentional. Struck at an early age with what would later be misdiagnosed in small children with boring parents as Obsessive Compulsive Disorder with Hyperactivity, Jefferies was forever looking for something to do. If there wasn't anything else to do, he'd clean, secure, and decorate his shop. In its early iteration, the garage had been fashioned in various styles including art deco, primitive, arts & crafts, postmodern, and for a brief time, contemporary Rasta style.

The transformations were really quite amazing, though disconcerting to the customers. It was one thing to walk into a service station and see a calendar depicting shirtless woman with a perpetually broken coverall strap. You'd rather expect that. It was quite another to see a Chat Noir poster, a framed M.C. Escher picture of two hands drawing each other, and a three-foot bong hanging on the wall on alternating weeks.

It was after a trip to a Famous Dave's Barbeque restaurant in Des Moines that Jefferies had settled on an early fifties garage motif. Unlike Famous Dave's, however, all of the Jefferies' bric-a-brac was authentically something he'd used over the years and not thrown out. Also, despite the worn and used look of every single curio in the collection, everything was scrupulously clean.

It was rare that Jefferies managed to sleep, which was a perfect trait for the one and only tow-truck operator in central Rhotic County. He didn't even bother posting hours on his door, or in the Yellow Pages ad. He just listed his cell phone number. It really didn't matter when customers called. He was nearly always ready.

The stranger's bike had been a mess. It was bent in delicate places, dented in the tougher ones, worked over in general, and scratched on most of the chrome surfaces. Some of that may have been how it was before it was defiled. It certainly hadn't seen a bug wash in at least two weeks. Kenneth Jefferies found its condition totally unacceptable. Fortunately, it was also just about the only project Jefferies had for the whole evening. There was painting the garage floor for the third time that month, but that could wait until at least three in the morning. A guy really does deserve to relax a little bit, especially when working on a beauty like this particular Speedmaster motorcycle. Someone bored out the motor, replaced the fuel control system with something he didn't recognize and didn't have any markings. Jefferies figured the bike had half-again the horsepower it sported coming off the factory floor. It was, however, rather abused at the moment.

He was wondering if he had enough stripper on the shelves when his phone rang. It had to be Denny from up in Colubra. He owned a cycle shop and had lots of parts. The question was, did he have Triumph parts. Jefferies had left a message for Denny before he even got back to the shop with the bike.

Jefferies picked up the digitalized 1940's payphone off the wall. "Hellowaddayawant?"

"Jefferies?" Denny said.

"You know it. How's it going Denny?"

"Fine Jefferies. I got your message."

"Yeah? Whatdajathink?"

"Barely understood it. You say you're looking for Triumph parts?"

"Yep'per. You got 'em?"

"I couldn't understand which ones you needed. Tell me again."

After returning to the shop, Jefferies had three minutes to kill between waxing a Pabst Blue Ribbon sign and knocking out a black belt Sudoku, so he had memorized the list of parts and their respective part numbers. As slowly as he could manage without being rude, Jefferies recited the list.

"I think I got it," Denny said after the entire litany had passed. "Unless I missed one or two, I should have all of these in stock. I'll have the parts to you tomorrow morning."

"Can you bring them tonight?"

"I suppose. Why so soon? Customer getting anxious?"

"No. I just..." Jefferies paused.

"Are you going to paint the floor again?"

"Yeah," Jefferies admitted, a bit embarrassed. His stellar work usually overshadowed his behavior, so people usually liked him. Still he didn't like telling people what he was planning, preferring to just do it.

"I see," Denny said. "What color are you going with this time?"

Jefferies brightened up. Denny was such a sport. "I'm thinking of doing a faux wood grain finish. It should look good with the oilcans and the red neon."

"Sounds just fine. Can't wait to see it." Denny paused for a second and then said, "Why the two different size oil filters?"

"I'm doing an oil change tonight too. Different bike. Another Triumph."

"Sounds like a good time. See you in about an hour and half."

"Good deal. See you in five thousand four hundred." Jefferies hung up the phone before Denny could say 'good-bye'. Jefferies hated good-byes.

In his dream, Chord was Frankenstein, or his monster. He couldn't remember which was which. Lightening ripped through his body. The table onto which he was strapped held him fast. The pain was incredible. Lights danced across his eyes, his jaw clenched so tight he thought he'd break his teeth. He heard his own guttural groan of pain, rage, and rebirth. He felt alive and like he was dying at the same time. Far below, he could hear the fiendish source of his pain cackle with the joyous victory of achievement.

"Rape! Rape! Holy Mother of God, protect me. Rape!"

"Sheezic Guurkist," Chord managed to say as he realized he was awake.

"Rape." Margret paused. "Wait. What did you say?"

Chord fell to the floor as Margret let off the trigger of the bright yellow Taser. Copper wires snaked from the front of the gun to two darts securely embedded in Chord's thighs.

Chord got up on one elbow. "I said, Jesus Christ lady. Why the hell would you Tase a sleep-"

Margret hit the button again. "Blasphemer! Blasphemer rape!"

She let up on the button five seconds later.

Chord had straightened when she hit the button a second time. Now, flat on his back, he felt it would be best not to move.

"You," said Dr. Frankenstein's mom, "Why don't you tell me just who you are? And keep civil tongue in your head or I'll make you bite it off."

Chord ventured a glance toward his feet. The woman was apple-shaped, probably about fifty-five, but dressed younger. She wore a dark flowered blouse, a calf-length skirt, and what looked like a calfskin leather jacket. She also wore an empty shoulder holster.

"My name is Michael Chord, ma'am. I fell asleep on the couch. May I get up now?"

"No. How come you're sleeping on the couch? You escape?" The woman gently wobbled, her head making a slow circle above her shoulders.

"Ma'am, are you drunk?"

"No. Just a bit tipsy. Shut up. You want to pee your pants? I could make that happen." Margret menaced the Taser again.

"I'm good. I'm good." Chord laid his head back down and looked at the ceiling.

"Where's the sheriff?" Margret drew out the 's' longer than necessary.

"Don't know. He left me here to sleep and make some phone calls."

"Not on the city dime, you don't."

"Relax." Chord was treading gently. "I used my cellphone."

"You mean this one?" Margret kicked the phone across the floor. It stopped next to his head. It was smashed. "Think you did that when you fell out of bed."

"Nice." Chord sighed. "May I get up now?"

"You gonna rape me?"

"No. I promise."

Margret put her hands on her hips. "Why not?"

Chord sat up a bit. Margret smiled a bit blurry-eyed smile.

"I'm just pulling your chain," she said. She walked over and pulled both of the darts out of Chords jeans with a quick tug. Chord yelped.

He scooted up to sit on the couch. He wasn't sure everything still worked and didn't want to risk standing.

"What's your name, and why are you in here, anyway?" Margret asked.

"My name is Michael Chord. I may have mentioned that. I stopped at Lucky's on my way through town tonight. While I was there, someone vandalized my bike. Sheriff Clark let me crash here until Jefferies at the shop gives me a call about my bike."

They both looked down at the busted cell phone.

"Doesn't look like that will happen," Margret said. "How 'bout you give me a lift home. I'll give you the keys. I live down the block from Kenny's shop.

"Besides," she added. "You might change your mind about raping me by the time we get there." She attempted a wink, but failed to limit the gesture to just one eye.

"I'd love to, Margret is it?" She nodded; her eyes closed and her penciled eyebrows rose. "But the sheriff still has my license."

"Why's he got that?"

"I take a great picture. I'm willing to chance the drive if you are."

"Sure, bet'cha."

"There wouldn't be a coffee shop on the way to your home, would there?"

"No."

"Shame. Well, we'll make it a quick trip." Chord took the spent Taser from Margret, wrapped the wires around the barrel, and set it on the counter. He herded her toward the exit.

Chord stopped, just as they got to the door.

"Hey," he said.

"What's that, Sweetie?" Margret asked, her hand reaching out for Chord's chest and missing.

"My headache is gone."

CHAPTER 7

ON THE ONE HAND, if Sydney Rollins hadn't left her travel purse in her room at the Nap 'N' Brekkers, she would have left with her two companions. On the other hand, had she left with the guys, she wouldn't have noticed the drain plug on her Rocket III had been tampered with and been able to call the tow truck to get it fixed. On the third hand, if she had left with the guys, she wouldn't be hanging from her arms in what she figured was the Morton building next to the Nap 'N' Brekkers. She certainly wouldn't be where she was now - hanging by her arms with her breasts exposed and getting very cold.

Just two hours earlier, Barry received a call from his contact. The courier wasn't coming through with the diamonds later on; he had already left. According to his contact, the courier did take the eastern route and agreed that Clements was a likely stopping place - unless the courier hadn't taken the diamonds through the town already.

Marty looked at Barry. "So what do we do now? Should we just keep going toward Anamosa like we planned and try to head him off there?"

"Unless he was really hauling ass, I doubt he

would have passed through already," Barry said. "But I think he'll be here soon." He clasped Marty's shoulder and looked at Sydney. "We have a real shot at this. If we find this guy, it is all a matter of distracting him while two of us shake down the bike."

"What if we don't find it?" Sydney asked. She wasn't entirely sure this sounded like a well-designed plan.

"Then we move it," Barry said.

"Steal the bike?"

"No, just move it somewhere we can get a better look at it; more time to find the diamonds. Once we find them, we leave the bike."

"It sounds good," Sydney admitted. "Who does what?"

"I think that is obvious," Marty said, getting into the spirit of the plan. "We'll need two guys to move the bike and one of us to distract our friend." He smiled at Sydney. "You, my dear, are the best distraction money could buy."

She'd always thought Marty had a nice smile for a guy so full of shit. At the moment, though, that smile far too smarmy to be attractive. "Is that why you're always riding drag when Barry takes point?"

"You know it. You can't beat the view."

They gathered their stuff, packing it quickly onto their bikes. They traveled light, which meant only the essentials. If they had to leave town in a hurry, they'd need their stuff with them. Each left two night's room and board money on their beds just in case they didn't come back. No use skipping out on the tab and attracting more heat.

Sydney was packing the last of her stuff when she noticed she'd forgotten her travel purse, of all things.

"I'm going back in," she told the guys. "I forgot something." She headed for the porch.

"Take your time," Marty called. "We'll ride on ahead. We want to get into town before you to check things out anyway." The two men fired up their bikes and turned out onto the road into town, their headlights cutting into the light fog of the night.

No one was in the house when she went upstairs to her room. In fact, since early that afternoon, they hadn't seen the tall, leggy woman who ran the place at all. That was fine with Sydney. The woman was too tall, too well built, and damn spooky.

After grabbing her purse, she returned to her bike. She planted her left foot to mount the machine, only to step in something wet. Sydney pulled a pocket flashlight from her cycle jacket and shined it at the driveway. A pool was spreading from under the oil pan.

She knelt down and checked the damage. The plug was loose, but twisted at an odd angle. Oil dripped from around the dangling bolt into a spreading pool.

"What the hell?" She said aloud.

She reached into her purse and pulled out the phone. In true biker fashion, she called information for a tow truck first. She'd call the cops after she knew her bike would be okay. The man at the tow service said he'd have a guy pick it up on his way into town in about half an hour.

"Thank you," she said. She disconnected and

took a moment to collect herself. Who the hell would do something like this? The plug certainly didn't fall out on its own. The guys wouldn't pull a stunt like this, even as a prank. In fact, it was going to be a wrinkle in their plans if she couldn't get into town soon. They needed her as the distraction: unless, of course, the courier was gay. It was then that it occurred to her, they didn't even know what the courier looked like.

"We had a hell of a time finding that plug." The voice startled Sydney. It came out of the shadow of the walnut tree in the front yard. "Did you know there are three plugs on that thing?"

The man in the shadows was rather large. He didn't have a discernible neck, but he had great diction.

"Who are you?" Sydney asked. "You did this?"

Her mind raced, relying on eight years of smuggling experience to find an escape. If that weren't enough to make a girl tough enough to bite chain and spit nails, growing up with four older brothers would certainly have prepared her for just about anything.

"Yep," said the shadow. "We had to make sure we got a chance to talk to you. We wouldn't want you running off before we could - get to know each other."

"Hey, we paid for the rooms. The cash is on the beds."

"I'm sure it is," the shadow said. "I'm sure it is. Only, we don't really care about that. We need some information."

"Like what?"

"First," the shadow said, "it's playtime."

A cloth fell in front of her face and down her torso. She tried to strike out, but her arms were restricted inside the bag. She screamed in rage as she felt the bear hug pin her arms and lift her off the ground. The grip was very strong, tightening after each exhalation. Eventually, she passed out.

When she awoke, she found herself in her current predicament - suspended from chains in what looked like a large garage. A table sat about ten feet in front of her. The desk lamp on the table shone directly at her, obscuring the two figures she could just make out behind the light. There was a large, red pickup parked next to her, and she could just make out various pieces of lawn equipment and tools on the wall to her right.

"Good morning," said one of the shadows on the other side of the lamplight. It didn't sound like the one from under the tree. It had to be the one who jumped her from behind.

She took stock of her condition. Her arms were secured apart and over her head with some kind of light chain. She could reach the floor with her boots if she put her legs together, but couldn't put them flat on the floor. She still had on her pants, but her jacket was splayed open by her outstretched arms. Her shirt and sport bra were ripped down the middle, exposing her C-cup assets. It was obvious to all she was cold.

Modesty was out of her reach, but there seemed no reason to panic. As near as she could tell, they hadn't molested her beyond a possible grope while she was unconscious. Taking a deep breath to clear her head, she faced the light and the shadows.

"What do you jerkwads want?" This was no time to be bashful. Maybe she could bully them. After all, they hadn't stripped her completely nude so there might be some decency in the shadows somewhere. If she was lucky, they might even be a little afraid. Maybe she could scare it to the surface.

"We told you," said the shadow from before. "We want some information."

"And you plan to torture me to get it?"

"Torture you," said the shadow in a strange voice, as if impersonating someone. "Torture you. That's good. It's a good idea. I like that." Sydney didn't get the reference.

The other shadow apparently did, because he laughed. "Harvey Keitel?" the second shadow asked. His voice was deeper.

"Yep. Pretty good, huh?"

"Yeah. That's pretty good."

"Hey," said the first voice. "I have a great idea for torturing the information out of her."

"Wait," said the first voice, but it was too late.

The first shadow made a quick movement. From out of the darkness, an orange blur hit the floor in front of Sydney before zipping past her ear.

"What the hell was that?" She demanded.

"Oh, that's good! Let me try one." A moment later a yellow blur hit the floor. This time, it bounced up and hit her in the forehead. It stung like a bitch, but didn't feel like it could do any actual damage.

"Ow!" She yelled. "What the hell was that?"

She caught another blur, a blue one this time.

John Montét

She kicked at it. She missed, but it hit her in the side of her jacket with a "fwap". A small blue ball fell and bounced off into the darkness. "Is that a SuperBall?"

She'd been distracted enough to miss the second orange one, which bounced up and hit her left breast, just on the edge of her areola.

"Ahh! That fucking stings, dammit! If you want information, how about asking some goddamned questions?"

A door opened behind the men. A tall, willowy shadow blocked the doorway. "They've been waiting for me. I ask the questions." The voice was feminine and familiar.

There was the distinctive sound of womanly heels on concrete as the shadow approached the men. She stopped before walking into the light.

The woman spoke quietly to one of the man shadows. "Why can I see her breasts?"

That's when she placed the voice.

"June?" Sydney asked.

"I'm so sorry you said that," June said, her voice dripping with mock pity. "Put the little balls away, Monty."

"Hey," Monty said, "You shouldn't use my actual name."

"Oh, I don't think that will be a problem," June said.

Sydney saw the last two feet of a bullwhip coil into the light.

CHAPTER 8

"RHAPSODE ALOYSIUS GONZAGA Abercrombie Morris the Third. Come here boy." Jairus had been calling the dog for some time and he was starting to become winded. It felt as if he was just going through the motions now. He figured that using Rhapsode's full given name made up in severity what he now lacked in volume.

While he knew nearly every lane in the county, it had been a while since he was this far up Turkey Road. The night was purple-dark, the clouds keeping the light of the gibbous moon from helping the situation. More than once he stumbled, releasing a string of Elizabethan-era cursing that would have made a badger blush. He only actually fell once.

It wasn't his body that hurt, however. It was his feelings. It is one thing to have a beautiful woman leave you while you slept. It is easy to accept that she would have better things to do. The world is a beautiful woman's oyster. It's a different matter with a dog. When a dog leaves you, especially a former companion and life-mate, it stings in a way that makes your stomach ache and your testicles tighten with worry. Heretofore, Rhapsode had never left his side for more than the call of nature, or a squirrel.

A squirrel. That's it, he thought. The interference of a sausage seemed unlikely; therefore, there must be a squirrel involved. The wayward spur-galled rapscallion had run off after one of those most vile arboreal rodentia and could be anywhere. There was nothing but trees around him. The whole valley was one big tree-rat highway.

"Rhapsode, you spleeny milk-jolted horn beast," he called. "Come to me. I'll not feed you a kibble for a fortnight if you do not appear this very instant."

No kibble takers appeared.

Jairus continued on. Eventually, Rhapsode would find his way back to the sanctum sanctorum of the grain bin in Clements, he hoped. It would be best to wait there. If the good Constable Clark were to once again rouse him, he would inquire as to the whereabouts of the local pound.

He'd not gone a score of steps with this thought when twin luminaries spread across the bend in the road ahead of him. He stepped off the road, into the ditch to avoid the oncoming automobile. In doing so, he stepped in a chilly puddle at the bottom of the ditch.

"Blast and damnation," he cried. "Will the fates kindly find other recourse to satisfy their chronic apathy?" He stepped back up onto the road.

As he did so, the car seemed to take notice of him and slow down. A rather nice Subaru stopped next to Jairus. It looked as though someone took the back-end off a station wagon in an effort to emulate a pickup truck. He remembered seeing it before. The driver behind the lowered window did not, however, look familiar.

"I'm supposed to ask you if you need a lift," said the driver. He was a youngish man. He wore a leather jacket and some kind of dark tee shirt. His face looked kind enough, if a bit scratched in the cheeks. He wasn't smiling.

"And who, pray tell, has given you this directive?"

"Hi Proof!" came an enthusiastic cry from the passenger seat. "Need a lift?"

Jairus squinted past the man to get a look at the passenger. He could just make out her form in the red light of the dashboard.

"Ms. Strangeland, I presume." Jairus knew Margret from the Sheriff's Office. He'd been fortunate enough to still be one of the few stationhouse regulars the woman hadn't Tased. He knew better than to correct her term of endearment. He'd been learning to live with it as of late, in any case.

"Hi ya," she called with a wave.

"In the spirits, I see. My envy runneth over."

"So, would you like a ride or not?" the man asked. "Proof, was it?"

"Dr. Jairus Dishome, at your service." Jairus did not bow but did extend a hand. "And you are?"

"Chord. Michael Chord," he said shaking Jairus' hand through the open car window.

"Ms. Strangeland's companion for the evening?"

"No, just her chauffer. I'm taking her home to sleep it off." Seeing the look on the old man's face, he added "I'll be walking to an appointment after I see her through the door."

"I see. You've honorable intentions then. Though I must inquire, why would you take on such an endeavor, my good man?" To Margret, "I mean no offense, Madam." She wasn't paying attention.

"This is her car. Besides the garage is just next door to her house. My ride is there."

"And which establishment would this be?"

"Don't know the name. It is the one owned by the tow truck guy, Jefferies."

"I'm afraid you've been duped, Sir. Mr. Jefferies's garage is in the opposite direction, back in the village. Your services are rendered in vain."

Chord swore softly and turned to Margret. Her head was tilted back, her mouth wide open toward the ceiling. "You lied to me," Chord said. "I'm going to borrow your car after I drop you off. I'll leave it at Jefferies's garage when I'm done. You can find your own ride there in the morning."

"Whatever," Margret said, not quite closing her smiling mouth.

Chord turned to Jairus. "You're going to have to show me where it is. I'm new around here."

"It would be my pleasure. I ask only that you drop me off at my normal hostel once you are done."

"Sounds like a plan." Chord hit the automatic locks to free the doors. Jairus declined.

"I prefer the open air to the prospect of witnessing another's regurgitation." Jairus swung himself into the bed of the Subaru Baja. He settled into a corner, clutching his pack to his chest. As the car began to move to turn around, Jairus scanned the night around them and wondered where Rhapsode could be.

For his part, Rhapsode was contentedly laying

on the floor of an RV, having his pasta-filled tummy scratched, even as a myriad of wonderful odors assaulted his nose. The old woman's RV was parked deep in the woods to the west of Clements and was full of all kinds of smells. A dog largely experiences his world through his nose. Though, like most dogs, Rhapsode was not usually judgmental of odor, this place was nearly overwhelming. The camper was the nasal equivalent of the attic of the Smithsonian after a tornado. It was almost too much to take in.

He had chased the perfumed squirrel when it finally darted out of the owl-hole tree and ran across the branches. It ran as if it knew exactly where it was going and exactly how to get there. Only once did it get within three feet of the ground, dipping when a branch partially broke under its weight, but it scrambled up and onward before Rhapsode could get to it.

Eventually, the road of tree branches stopped over the parked RV and the squirrel hopped onto the roof. It looked down at its pursuer, chattering admonishments whose meanings Rhapsode couldn't quite understand (squirrels never make any sense), before disappearing past the roof's edge. He barked insults and challenges in an effort to get it to come back.

When the old woman had opened the door at the sound of his barking, Rhapsode forgot about the squirrel. The smells washed over his nose like the contents of Fibber McGee's closet. The scents spilled down the steps and across the grass, burying him in so much information, he actually yelped. A moment later he was absolutely enthralled. Rosemary, thyme, wax, a touch of mildew, cilantro, and something pickled all roiled over the scent of rat and squirrel. Cooked things tumbled with rotting fruit, warm tomatoes, and sprouting potatoes. Hints of must and mold merged with burnt wood, crushed apple, hot water, and some kind of bird. Perhaps it was pheasant. There were human smells too. Sweat, woman smells, and a touch of blood all mingled with at least a hundred different toiletry products. There were perfumes, cleaners, and candles all assaulting his now overwhelmed nostrils.

"Well," the lady had said. "You want some dinner or not? I can't stand here all day, and the spaghetti is getting cold."

Rhapsode looked around just a bit before climbing wide-nostrilled up the steps and into the RV.

Ten minutes later, he was so enthralled by the smells and the old woman's expert scratching he hadn't notice the heavily scented doe squirrel in a cage by the window. She was watching a nearly exhausted off-season suitor sitting on a birdfeeder just outside the window.

The whip cracked again, this time snapping around to the back of Sydney's thigh.

"Ahh!" she screamed. Even though the whip didn't actually tear her heavy jeans, she knew the blows were raising welts. She figured thighs and ass must look like embarrassed zebra skin under her denim.

June Williams coiled the whip again, letting it snake around the concrete floor. She tried to decide if it was time to start working on the woman's exposed breasts. She'd been saving them as a last resort. She wanted to see if she could get her information before starting to mark up what she had to admit was a rather nice rack.

"So," June said stroking the first bend of the whip like a pet snake, "what exactly does this guy look like? What's the courier's name? I really don't think you should be holding out on me, do you?"

"I don't know, I'm telling you," Sydney sniffled. She wasn't crying, but the whip had certainly made her eyes water. She was trying to go with it. This Williams bitch would think she was breaking if she started crying.

Being mostly clothed and worked over with a whip wasn't exactly torture to Sydney. It sure as hell wasn't fun, but she'd gone through worse. Much worse. Many years before, three men once tortured her for an entire night taking turns berating her, spitting in her face, and once even punching her in the stomach. They forced her to spend a night gagged and tied to a chair in an exceptionally cold basement wearing nothing but her underwear. They hadn't sexually molested her, of course. They did, however, leave the television in the room was tuned to a Nickelodeon marathon of Leave it to Beaver. To this day, she breaks out in hives at the sound of a muted trumpet. Brothers can be such forgetful assholes.

"That, I'm afraid that is just unacceptable. I know

about the diamonds. I know your friends got the call from your connection. I know you are their leader. That means you have the details that I don't."

"I'm not the leader. What makes you think I'm the leader?" She tried to let a whine creep into her voice. To her it sounded like a pathetic attempt. She just wasn't a shrinking violet. June didn't seem to notice the insincerity.

"I know you're the leader," June said. "Do you have any idea how many riders come through Clemens each year? Hundreds. If there are two things I've learned, they are that most Harley Riders have disposable income and that the leader rides the biggest bike. Yours is what, 1,800 CC's?"

"2,300."

"No shit? Well, that is certainly the biggest bike I've ever seen under a skinny little bitch like you. So that makes you the leader of your little group. That means you have the information I need. So spill it, or things are going to get a bit more nippy in here."

Sydney snapped her head up as she caught the inference.

June turned to one of the shadow men. "Monty, give her another ball."

"What color?" Monty asked.

"It doesn't fucking matter what color. Just bounce another fucking ball."

As the smaller shadow, Monty, moved to grab another ball, June drew the whip back into the darkness. Monty threw the ball hard against the concrete in front of Sydney. As it came up to her, the whip lashed out, splitting the ball in two. Both halves of the ball bounced off her sternum with very little force, and dropped to the floor.

"Oh fuck" Sydney breathed.

The two shadowed men chuckled.

"Now then," June said, coiling the whip back into the darkness. "Let's see about that little left nipple of yours."

Panic shot through Sydney. Her right hand had been loosened since a shot to the inside of her thigh had made her screech and jog on her tiptoes. She had been waiting until someone got too close before unwrapping it and kicking some ass, but the thought of the whip hitting her nipple sparked her to action.

She saw June move as if to strike. Kicking her elbow out, she shook off the chain encircling her right wrist. She grabbed her left wrist, lifted her feet, and used the chain to swing into the darkness. The whip cracked just behind her.

Sydney swung smoothly across the floor, knees up, until coming to a resounding thud against the door of a big red truck parked just outside the lamplight. She quickly stood, shaking her hand desperately, trying to shake off the chain on her left wrist. It was hopelessly tangled.

She could hear her captors yelling for her to stop as they came across the floor toward her.

Fuck it, she thought. The door to the truck was unlocked. She opened it and swung her arm over the top of the door as she hopped into the truck. She slammed the door on the chain, and locked the door. The chain, the decorative kind used to hold bird feeders and plant baskets, hadn't broken.

The two men reached the door and started pulling on the handle.

"Go the fuck around to the other side," said the large man.

Sydney lunged to hit the lock on the other door, but her wrist was trapped near the top of the driver's door. She couldn't reach the lock.

As she watched, Monty rounded the front of the car. He slipped on something, but caught himself on the hood.

Then it occurred to her; power locks.

She hit the button on her door just as Monty got to the door handle.

"It's locked, Jed."

Sydney instinctively reached for the key in the ignition - and found it. The truck cranked over immediately and roared under the weight of Sydney's foot. She slammed it into reverse. The rear tires squealed and smoked for a moment before the truck lurched backward three feet into the garage door. Her wrapped hand was yanked painfully into the roof of the truck.

Monty and Jed both ducked for cover.

"Shoot the bitch," June yelled. "Shoot her!"

Sydney threw the truck into drive, crashing into a riding lawnmower before hitting the brakes. She was tossed forward into the steering wheel by the impact, but wasn't hurt. She spotted a garage door opener on the passenger visor and hit the button. The overhead light came on as the door started to open behind her.

She threw the car into reverse again and punched it.

The garage door was only partway up when she hit it. It crashed against the back of the cab, shattering the rear and passenger windows as the truck crashed through, splintering the lower garage door panel. The chain gave a quick and painful yank on Sydney's left arm before the links snapped.

Sydney hurled backward until she was past the driveway and on to the highway beyond. She hit the brakes again. Through the windshield she saw the three of them duck under the broken door to stand in the driveway looking at her - two men of different sizes and a tall woman holding a whip - all silhouetted in front of the lamplight in the garage sixty feet away. None of them looked like they were holding a gun. Quickly, she opened the door and pulled in the eight feet of chain dangling outside. She threw it on her lap and spun out down the road toward Clements.

The three stood, not moving or speaking, watching the lights of the truck disappear into the night.

After a moment, June spoke in an even tone. "Kindly explain why you didn't shoot her." She kept her eyes looking after the truck.

"We don't have any real guns," Monty said. "Just the BB guns. They're in the trunk of the Nova."

June sighed. "We'll have to bring a pair of mine then, won't we?"

"You know where she's going?" Jed asked.

This had been exhausting. It wasn't the damage, or the fact that they still didn't know how to find the courier, or the diamonds. She felt drained from the sudden loss of control and a little turned on by the whipping. When this was all over, she was going to have to call up Virgil Ferris for a session. Then she could gain back her control. Besides, he owed her a favor. After laundering all her money through his grocery store accounts, he'd made a small fortune. She was still thinking about what she was going to do to Virgil when she realized the two of them were staring at her.

"Of course I know where she is going," June said. She turned and started back to the house, her heels clipping loudly as she went to get her gun. "She's going back to get her bike."

Sydney was glad she hadn't run into a cop on the way from the Nap 'N' Brekkers. She wasn't about to go over the events of the last hour with authorities - not yet, anyway. The first order of business was to find Barry and Marty. You would have thought they would have come for her. You would have thought two reasonably sane bastards would have kicked down the door, kicked some ass, and helped a girl find a new shirt.

Fuckers.

Sydney wasn't really mad at them. She was just mad. Her stress level ran way too high. Adrenalin was turning her into a hormonal nightmare. Ass would have to be kicked at some point.

She came down the north hill into Clements way too fast. Three blocks later, she spied her companion's bikes. They had parked on a side street, around the corner from a place called Heaven's Kitchen Supper Club. She drove fast enough to squeal the tires as she rounded the corner toward the bikes. For a moment, she considered running over the motorcycles out of spite, but decided instead to pull up in the empty side street behind them.

Marty and Barry walked around the corner behind Heaven's Kitchen as she threw the truck in park and killed the lights. She threw open the door and stormed up to the two of them.

"Where in the fuck were you guys?" She pushed them both in the chest, hard.

Neither said a word. They were both standing still, their mouths agape.

"I said, where the fuck were you?" She put her hands on her hips. "Why would you just fucking leave me there? Why didn't you come back for me?"

They didn't move. Sydney followed their gaze down to her still-exposed chest and then glared back to their faces. "Eyes up, gentlemen."

They both snapped out of it, popping their eyes to look directly straight ahead. "What the hell happened to you, Sydney?" Marty asked.

"That witch back at the B & B and her two thugs happened, that's what." She folded her arms under her breasts, daring them to look again. "She was asking about the courier and the diamonds." They were staring at her forehead trying like hell not to look down or into her eyes.

"How'd she know about them?" Marty asked.

"No fucking idea," Sydney snapped. "Where were you?"

"We've been here this whole time. Waiting to see if this Chord guy shows up," Barry said.

"Chord?"

"Yeah. We made some calls. That's the guy's name. Mike Chord. He does runs like this for the agency, but no one saw him since he left the cities. We know he rides a Speedmaster. We've been on the lookout, but haven't caught sight of him."

Marty spoke up. "We saw your bike."

Sydney looked at him. She respected Marty, but if he so much as smiled, she'd deck him. "Where did you see my bike?"

"It was on a flatbed," Barry said. "It turned down a street about two blocks up."

"And you didn't think that maybe, just maybe, I was in trouble?"

Barry looked at his feet and stroked his chin. "That would have been a logical conclusion, I suppose. Honestly, though, we figured you were in the tow truck."

In all the years Sydney had ridden with Barry, he never seemed to get alarmed when faced with obvious issues. She always thought it was because he could think well under stress. Now she was beginning to think he just didn't have the brains.

"Well, let's go get my bike," Sydney said over her shoulder on her way back to the truck.

"What about the courier?" Marty asked.

"First we get my bike." She hopped into the cab. "Then we find the courier. Both of you - get in the back. There is glass on the passenger seat."

As they walked, Barry turned to Marty. "What makes her think she can push us around?"

"She has the bigger bike," Marty replied. "And tits."

CHAPTER 9

IT WAS HARD FOR CHORD TO BELIEVE just how easily Margret fooled him. As he turned down Maunder Avenue toward the garage, he realized he had actually read the address on the side of Kenneth Jefferies' truck when he'd picked up his bike. He had committed it to memory at the time, but it hadn't occurred to him until now. It must have been the Taser. The damn thing must have scrambled parts of his brain.

They had dropped Margret off at her house several miles away. They didn't leave until they saw the light go on in an upstairs room - presumably as she flopped onto her bed. The vagrant professor was sitting the passenger seat now, his pack on his lap, giving Chord directions. He smelled of old patchouli and cloves with a touch of whiskey.

"It's just up here, Mr. Chord."

He had already spotted the sign - a highly polished and waxed piece of engraved steel jutting from the side of an otherwise nondescript single-story building. It read "K.J.'s House of Grease." The cinderblock building sported a freshly painted textured brown. The three rows of blocks nearest the foundation were painted a deep and complementary red. The doorframes and windowpanes stood out, radiating the same crimson shade. Stylized yellow and red painted flames crawled up the sides of the plate glass window. Arching white letters repeated the name of the shop. A pig wearing pinstriped overalls and an engineer's cap waved to the viewer just below the letters.

"Does Jefferies serve food here?"

"Not as I am aware," Jairus said. "Why do you ask such a thing?"

"No reason. I'm just suddenly hungry."

Jairus reached into his pack and started to rummage. "Allow me, then, to offer you a sandwich."

"Thank you, no." Chord said. He liked the guy, but he wasn't about to eat anything that came out of that pack.

"Very well then," Jairus said. "Perhaps another time."

Chord pulled into the parking lot. He spotted the flatbed truck onto which they had loaded the bike earlier. It was empty. He took that as a good sign.

Parked next to it was another flatbed tow truck. This one was from a bike shop in Colubra according to the painted logo on the door. That was another good sign, unless the damage was so great that Jefferies needed help.

He parked the car and turned to Jairus. "Say, now that I know where to find this place, can I give you a lift to your... where you'd like to go?"

Jairus shook his head. "Thank you for offering, my good man, but I shall manage just fine. The constitution does well in the open air. I'm afraid I can no longer stand the confines of an automobile." He popped open the door and extended a hand. "Good evening to you, sir."

Chord shook his hand. The man's grip was astoundingly firm. "Good evening to you as well."

He stepped out of the car with Jairus and watched the man shoulder his pack and walk away. Then Chord went inside the House of Grease.

"You're all fixed up, there," Jefferies said handing the bike key back to Chord.

Chord ran his hand over the machine. He couldn't believe it. The bike looked as good as new. The hole in the tank was gone. The scratches were buffed out. Both foot pegs had been replaced, including the right side peg he'd bent when he slipped into a curb a little too hard several weeks before. Even the tank emblems had been repaired, or replaced. He honestly couldn't tell which.

"Are you sure it is my bike?" Chord asked. "You sure you didn't just have your friend here bring down a new one?"

Jefferies stood next to Denny Huber. The two were beaming.

"He's sure," Denny said. "We don't even keep Triumph bikes in stock at my shop. We just keep a few parts on hand for repairs. It didn't take much."

"Didn't take much?" Chord asked. "The bike was a wreck."

"Kenny likes to fabricate most of his parts when he has the material. That tank of yours has been welded and painted."

"The last clear coat need to cure a bit more,"

Jefferies said. "Didn't have enough time to bake it all the way."

"You have a paint booth and heat room here?"

"Naw," Jefferies said. "I just free-handed the logos and put it in the Kenmore in the kitchen. It goes up to 800 degrees if I need it to."

"Really?"

"Well, I've tweaked it a bit."

Chord was duly impressed. Jeffries did some amazing work done in a ridiculously short timeframe. Now he wished he hadn't called Jack Dockage. He could have made the trip to Waterloo after all. It was too late now, however. Jack was on his way and his cellphone, with Jack's number, was in pieces. He'd have to keep the bike here, out of sight, until Jack left. Otherwise, Jack was likely blow a flipping gasket.

Denny said his goodbyes and left, leaving Chord and Jefferies to settle up.

"Are you very sure you didn't just buy a new bike?" Chord asked, staring at the bill. He was still staring as he handed his credit card to Jefferies.

"I'm sure. You needed a lot of parts, Mister. I only charged you $150 for the labor. Recalibrating the injectors was my idea."

Chord looked up. "You recalibrated the injectors?"

"Yep. I figured I got you almost a second off your quarter-mile. Might drop your mileage a little bit, so I repacked your mufflers."

Jefferies ran the card and handed it back to an open-mouthed Michael Chord.

"Hey," Jefferies said holding up both hands.

"You ain't mad are you? 'Cause if you are I can put most of it back the way it was. But it's going to take at least another hour and I'm not sure I remember where all the scratches were and I don't know what to do about the bugs but I suppose I could take it for a-"

"Stop. Just stop," Chord interrupted. "I'm not pissed. I'm just astounded."

Jefferies looked at him with confused eyebrows.

"Thank you, Jefferies. I appreciate your work. It is simply astonishing."

Jefferies smiled. "I almost forgot," he said. "I found this." He reached into his pocket and pulled out the little black leather sack of diamonds. He handed it to Chord.

Oh shit, thought Chord. This severely complicates things.

"You know," Jefferies said, "I understand you wanting to keep the flash drive safe, but I don't think the glass beads are good for it."

"Pardon?"

"Your flash drive - the one in with all the glass beads. It will really get banged up if you keep riding with it in there."

Chord opened the bag. Inside weren't the diamonds he'd expected. Instead, he saw two-dozen or so clear glass beads, the kind used in flower arranging. Nestled inside the beads was a rectangular, black USB flash drive.

What the fuck, he thought.

"Where are the diamonds, Jefferies?" Chord looked him dead in the eye.

Jefferies eyes grew wide again. "I didn't see any

diamonds, Mr. Chord."

"Michael."

"Michael. I swear I didn't find any diamonds. Were they in another bag?" He stepped back as Chord slowly advanced.

"There was only the one bag, Jefferies. There was only one secret compartment, only one bag, and at least five million dollars' worth of diamonds."

He was just inches from Jefferies face, having backed him against the register. "I am working for some very bad men, Kenneth - very bad men indeed. They are expecting the diamonds in just a few hours. If they don't diamonds, they will do unspeakable things to me Kenneth - very unspeakable things. So, I'm going to ask you again, Kenneth. Where the hell are the diamonds?"

Jefferies fell apart. He started talking so fast Chord could only catch bits and pieces.

"...I checked every tube when I did my frame measurements...

"...wouldn't take candy from a desk jar without asking...

"...help you look but I know I didn't drop anything, would have heard them if they spilled..."

Shit, thought Chord. He really doesn't have them.

"Okay, Jefferies," Chord said, backing away.

"...had known there were diamonds I would have put down a cloth..."

"Okay, Jefferies."

"...I don't deal with pain so make it quick if you can..."

"Jefferies!"

"...gone to church in years but could have now..."

Chord was going to have to try another tactic. "Nipple clamps!" he yelled.

"...with a garden hose- Wait. What?" Jefferies looked at Chord. The spell was broken. Then he gasped, "you're not going to-"

"No, no," Chord said. "I just had to hit you with a non sequitur so you'd stop. Works better than a slap."

"I suppose it does," Jefferies said.

He put his hand on Jefferies' shoulder. The mechanic flinched. "Look, I'm sorry Jefferies. I just panicked a bit. I know you didn't take anything."

Jefferies looked remarkably relieved.

"Think for a moment," Chord said. "Is there any chance someone could have swapped out the bag before you had a chance to look inside?"

Jefferies pursed his lips in thought. "Not a chance. I looked in the bag right away. I thought you might have been transporting dope. There wasn't anything in the bag but glass beads and that flash drive. I swear."

The situation smelled very bad. Chord didn't look in the bag when he picked it up in the Twin Cities, so he hadn't seen the actual diamonds. It was like every other package and he had no reason to think otherwise. It was all completely normal. Hell, the whole run felt normal before he stopped at Lucky's.

Why would his connection, a jewelry broker in St. Paul, pay him $50,000 to transport a flash drive? Could the real package have been stolen at a gas stop? If so, why would they leave a flash drive behind? Could it have been included so the bag

John Montét

would feel the same? If so, that would leave one question.

"Where the fuck is it?" a feminine voice bellowed from behind them.

Jefferies and Chord turned to see a petite woman standing in the doorway, a hand on each side of the doorframe. She was wearing motorcycle boots and her jeans were tiger-striped with black marks. As they watched, a piece of safety glass fell from her hair, rolled down shoulder of her open coat, and bounced off one of her bared breasts.

"I'll ask again." The woman actually panted with rage. "Where the fuck is my bike?"

Sheriff Clark pulled traffic duty in the hours just after dusk. He sat in his cruiser just off the main road, at the bottom of the hill south of town. The car lay nearly invisible in the twilight, tucked neatly behind a tree Clark remembered climbing when he was young. The tree seemed huge then. Now, it appeared twice as large, towering nearly 80 feet into the air. Its large trunk and its location at the edge of the floral shop parking lot made for perfect cover. Not that Clark really had his heart in handing out tickets. It was just something he had to do. That night, however, it was a point of normality in an otherwise strange day.

He'd managed to stop a number of speeders coming down the steep hill into town. Most just didn't see the speed limit sign at the top of the hill.

This, in point of fact, was by design. The city council hired a DOT representative to show the local road crew the best and worst spots to place the sign. After reading the report, the council opted for the later. It was a matter of fiscal responsibility, they said.

Clark's contract stated that while he didn't have an actual quota of tickets each day, he did have a responsibility to generate a certain level of revenue each quarter. It was the aspect of the job he cared for least, so he adopted a time-honored tradition among small town law enforcement; he targeted out of state license plates. He stopped just enough locals to make the record books seem more statistically normal, but local residents usually just received warnings. There was no point in making enemies in a town the size of Clements.

He was taking a radar break in the dark cruiser by surfing the federal alert websites on his laptop. Clark didn't actually harbor dreams of becoming a federal officer, but ever since Deputy Harlan Overgaard seized that drug fugitive in Deerburg, he had to admit to a bit of jealousy. It wasn't that Overgaard had made the papers, or that the governor had given him a formal accommodation that gave Clark a bit of envy. It was that Overgaard had managed to do a bit of definitive good for the community. Neil Clark often felt that he was just keeping the peace and maintaining the status quo. So, he surfed the federal alerts whenever he had a chance. It obviously paid to stay informed.

He was about to give it up and head back to the station when a car shot past the front of the cruiser. It went by in a dark blur - without its lights on. His radar read 25 miles an hour. The speed limit dropped to 45 here. The blur was moving at least twice that speed, perhaps 100 miles per hour. The car must have a radar blocker, which was illegal most states, including Iowa.

He hit his lights and siren, spinning his tires in the gavel of the parking lot as he pulled out onto the highway. The cruiser rounded the corner, still accelerating. Clark was able to see the highway for almost two miles as it dropped into Clements. There was only one car visible, and it had its lights on. It also didn't appear to be speeding. There was no dark blur, no speeding vehicle. There were, however, new black marks on the highway about a quarter mile behind the seemingly sluggish car. As Clark's cruiser approached, the car pulled over onto the shoulder. The beige Toyota Camry sported in-state license plates. It didn't seem capable of the speed he just witnessed. Still, it was the only car on the road. If it wasn't the speeding vehicle, it had to at least have seen where the speeder had gone. He pulled behind the car and ran the plates.

It took just twenty seconds to come back with the registration. The database listed one Ms. Shard Jandal of Dubuque as the registered owner. It listed no warrants, alerts, or prior arrests for Ms. Jandal. Her record was clean. The registration information also stated that the car was white, not beige. While this could mean the plates were stolen or it could be simply a clerical error. Clark made a note to run the VIN.

He stepped out and approached the driver's side of the car with professional caution. He could see the driver had the window down and had both hands on the wheel. He shined the flashlight into the window. The light glared off the driver's thick glasses. He had short, close-cropped hair, and wispy stubble that looked more intentional than careless. This was certainly not Ms. Shard Jandal.

"What would be the problem, officer?" The man said in a nasal, almost comical tone.

"This is just a routine check, Sir. May I see your license, registration, and insurance information?"

"Certainly." The man turned without taking his hands from the wheel. "Here you go, sheriff." A third hand appeared between the other two. It held something with a barrel as large and big around as a soup can.

Sheriff Neil Clark had just enough time to register that the right arm was fake before the pain exploded in his chest and everything went very, very black.

CHAPTER 10

TIFFANY WALKED HOME FROM PRACTICE, her Ibanez bass guitar slung in a gig bag over her shoulder. Practice hadn't gone well. Emetic Kitten suffered from general lack of angst and it showed in nearly every song. In fact, they all sucked. The guitar player was just learning to improvise in the high school jazz band and kept slipping little jazz phrases into "Your Love is My Bedsore". It completely ruined the spirit of the song. The keyboard player couldn't lay off the pitch bender so their best ballad, "Effluence of My Heart", took on a decidedly Devo air. The drummer - well, she just had a bad case of Drummer's Disease. Science had yet to discover a treatment, let alone a cure.

Tiffany, Emetic Kitten's visionary bass player (watch your ass, Les Claypool) was just as distracted. In her case, it was sub-routine transformations across a Base16 matrix. A simple conversion to hexadecimal simply couldn't cause an accumulative error. It just couldn't, okay? During the mile and a half back walk back to her house, she kept missing turns as she wrote, erased, and rewrote code in her head. It was a good thing practice got out early.

She just about reached Main Street when she

smelled a car coming.

It was one of those weeks where her sense of smell really kicked in (for three days a month she couldn't bring herself to even contemplate chicken salad). Even if it hadn't been one of those weeks, she would have been able to smell the RV from two blocks away. Certainly, she would have heard it. It rattled and popped its way down the hill toward her. Through the windshield, she saw shadows swaying and sparkling reflections dancing under the interior light.

She could see an old lady laughing maniacally in the driver's seat with octogenarian glee. It looked like Ella Pierce. Tiffany recognized her from the old woman's monthly visits to the Fareway grocery store during which she would buy tons of strange produce and boxes and boxes of dry pasta. Tiffany and the rest of the employees could always tell when Ella was in the store by the clangs of the cart hitting the shelves. You could track her progress from anywhere in the store by following the cries of "ouch", and "hey" that rose from the aisles. She was the sole reason Mr. Ferris forbade stocking glass items on the third shelf. The idea of Ella driving something as large as an RV, on public highways, was nothing short of terrifying.

As the RV passed, she saw a dog sitting in the passenger seat. It looked like Rhapsode, Old Proof's dog. He was sitting up on the seat, his head sticking out of the passenger window, a big panting smile spread across his doggie face. The rattling vehicle rocketed by with a smell that reminded Tiffany of an Italian family's compost heap dumped behind the perfume counter at Walgreen's by a wet donkey smoking a pipe.

When the RV passed under a streetlight, she saw something clutching to the top of the roof. In a moment, she realized it was a squirrel. She loved squirrels! The poor thing was going to get hurt riding on top of that deathtrap!

She ran after it, making it half a block before tripping on a raised piece of sidewalk. She went down, skidding on the concrete and giving her knee a serious case of road rash. She sat up and clutched at her wounded knee. The pain made her rock back and forth while sucking air through her teeth. Still she called after the RV.

"Ssssst, Ella! Ssssst, Ella!"

"Are you all right, young maiden?" said a voice from behind her. She saw the Old Proof loping up the sidewalk. She shrugged off the gig bag setting the bass aside. She started to try to get up and didn't want to fall and risk breaking the instrument.

"Just sit down, young lady," Jairus said as he reached her side. "Let's have a look at that knee."

"No really, Proof. I'm fine." She winced and sat back down hard. "Ah!"

"It is evident that you are not fine in this regard. Kindly sit still and let me see what I can find."

Tiffany didn't argue. She watched as the Old Proof dug around in his pack.

"It is pronounced 'prof', by the way."

"What?"

"Prof. It is short for professor. 'Proof' simply won't do in this case."

"Oh. Sorry."

"You may call me Jairus. My teaching days are long behind me."

"Okay."

Jairus reached into his worn pack and pulled what looked like a brand new first aid kit, a three-quarters full bottle of Pappy Van Winkle's, and a neatly folded small blanket. He handed her the thin blanket.

"What's this for?" Tiffany asked.

"Your dignity. You'll have to bend your knee while I work on it."

"So?"

"You're wearing a skirt, my dear."

"Oh," she said. She strategically draped the blanket. It was clean and smelled softly of hippy soap.

The Prof worked quickly and with a practiced hand. In no time he cleaned her wound with the bourbon (skillfully avoiding soaking her sock in booze), applied a Neosporin smeared 4x4, and wrapped it in place with a self-adhesive cloth bandage. It was even orange!

"Thanks, Prof," she said.

"You are welcome my dear." Jairus stood up. "I must be off."

"Hey," Tiffany said as he helped her to her feet. "I saw your dog."

"Truly? Pray, tell. Where is he?"

I saw him in Ella Pierce's RV. They just drove past. I was trying to catch them when I fell.

The old man looked relieved and excited. "Did you by chance see in which direction they went?"

"Sure. She turned down the street toward

Jefferies' place."

"I was there not an hour ago." Jairus shouldered his pack and headed after the RV at a fast walk. "A thousand times I thank you, kind lady."

As she watched Jairus leave, she remembered the squirrel clinging to the top of Ella's RV. What if the squirrel and fallen? Damn it, she would never forgive herself if she didn't do something.

"Hey," Tiffany called after Jairus, "There was a squirrel. On the roof. Make sure it is okay." Jairus gave no indication he' heard her. He was probably too deaf and too far away to hear.

Shouldering her bass again, she limped on after the Old Prof.

Chord could tell this was not a woman to trifle with. Perhaps the same thing could be said of all scowling bare-chested women. This one looked as if she had been through the ringer. Red lines and welts rose on her stomach. Black streaks crossed the thighs of her jeans. Her breathing was heavy and deep, as if she had just run a quarter-mile. The intensity and anger in her eyes reminded Chord of a wounded mountain lion. He sincerely hoped Jefferies had her bike.

"Eyes up gentlemen," she said. Chord and Jefferies immediately looked up, intentionally fixing their eyes on her forehead. Sydney Rollins let go of the doorframe, strode into the office, and crossed an arm over her chest, finally breaking the spell for

Jefferies.

"Your bike?" he said. "Would that be the Rocket?"

"Yes, it would. Where is it?"

"It's in the shop. No one was there when I picked it up; oil all over the place. I drained the rest of it and replaced the plug. I had to re-tap the threads though. Someone cross threaded the bolt."

"Did they." She said. It wasn't a question.

"I didn't have time to do anything else to it."

"What else would you have done?"

"Don't get him started," Chord interrupted.

Jefferies was still having a hard time maintain eye contact with Sydney. He cleared his throat and said, "I'll go get your bike and pull it out front."

They both watched him go. Sydney turned back to Chord.

"You mind?" She asked, pointing with her free hand to several stacks of black "House of Grease" tee shirts.

Chord handed her one off the stack of smalls. She took it and turned to face the window away from him. She took off her jacket, placing it on the counter in front of her, then shrugged off the remnants of her torn shirt and sport bra. Before pulling the shirt over her head, she extended her hand toward the window and flipped off two men sitting in the back of the red truck in which she arrived. Both men smiled and turned away.

"Friends of yours?" Chord asked.

"Just barely," she said putting on her coat. She threw the torn clothes in the trash.

"You've seen more of me than a strange man

should," she said. "I ought to at least know your name. I'm Sydney Rollins." She stuck out her hand.

He reciprocated the handshake. "Michael Chord. Pleased to meet you, Sydney."

Chord saw her eyes momentarily widen, just a little bit, before she regained composure. It wasn't a good sign. She knew his name, but not his face. That only meant one thing. She and her friends were fellow smugglers. This could get sticky.

"Pleased to meet you too. Mr. Chord, was it?"

"Michael, please."

"Michael."

Sydney wandered to the windowed door leading to the garage shop. As she walked, Chord could tell she was doing so with deliberate slowness and just a little extra wiggle in her hips. It meant that she wanted something and was buying time, probably to think of a strategy.

"That your Speedmaster in there?"

"Yep."

"It looks brand new."

"I've had my suspicions lately that it is. Otherwise, Jefferies does amazing work. You should let him keep your bike for a few more days. He might even repack your tailpipe for you."

Sydney spun around to face him. "He might what?"

"Sorry," Chord said. "I should have said repack your muffler. He says it improves your mileage."

"That didn't sound any better. I think I'll pass." She walked to the door leading outside. "Well, I see he has my bike out front. I must be off."

Over her shoulder, Chord could see Jefferies was

talking with her two companions. It looked as if the two of them were prodding Jefferies for information. Chord had no idea if Jefferies could take another round of intimidation. He'd have to do something to head all of this off.

Sydney started to open the door.

"You can have them, if you want," he said.

She stopped, but didn't turn around. "And what would that be?" she asked.

"The diamonds."

Sydney froze. "What diamonds would those be?"

"That syntax really gets old fast. You know perfectly well what diamonds I'm talking about."

Sydney turned to face him. "What exactly are you talking about? How would I know about any diamonds?"

"Three reasons, really. First, it is obvious by the state of your dress when you walked in here that you've been through hell tonight. That fact is substantiated by the condition of your truck and the fact that all of you drove here on four wheels even though you are all still dressed for two.

"That leads me to the second reason. Considering your companions' attire, you are all bikers. There is no reason, absolutely no reason at all, for three riders to stop in this town unless there is specifically something here for them. My stopping here was a regrettable fluke."

Sydney started opened her mouth to protest. Chord pointed a finger at her nose to stop her.

"Thirdly," he continued, "I could tell that you recognized my name. I've never seen you at the family reunions, and we've never dated. I can assure you I would have remembered a set as nice as yours. Your green eyes, I mean."

Sydney blushed a bit despite herself.

"That means you knew my name from an acquaintance. If you know people I know, then I know that you know what they know, which means you know what I do. You know what I mean?"

"Not at all," she said.

"Well, then there is this." Chord reached into his jacket pocket and pulled out the small black bag. He made a move to hand it to her, but dumped the contents on the floor.

"No!" she cried. Sydney dropped, trying to catch the stones as they fell. She squatted on the floor to sweep them up, stopping only when she realized they were just glass beads. Chord had removed the flash drive earlier.

"There really aren't any diamonds?" she asked staring at a handful of sparkling aquarium material.

"If there were, I never had them. Someone is either testing me by sending me on a dry run, or they are just fucking with me."

"How do I know you didn't just hide the diamonds somewhere?"

"Fuck!"

"I beg your pardon?" she asked.

"I said 'Fuck'." Chord was looking past her into the parking lot. "You want proof?" He stepped past her, threw open the front door, and rushed outside.

Jefferies was quite obviously upset. His hands were in the air, and he looked scared as hell. For their part, Sydney's two companions were completely taken aback by the stream of consciousness Jefferies was hurling at them. It was a defense mechanism reminiscent of a horned toad. The difference was, while a horned toad squirts blood at his attackers, Jefferies squirted his own confusion.

"Boob job!" Chord yelled at the top of his lungs.

Twenty minutes later, over coffee (Jefferies only stocked decaf) Chord explained the situation to the three of them. While the three companions confessed to wanting to steal the diamonds, they hated to see a colleague get screwed like Chord had just been.

"So," Chord asked Sydney. "Are you ready to spill your story for the evening? Let's start with who really owns the truck with the busted windows."

"I'm telling you, it is just not possible."

June Williams was not having a good evening. First there was the fiasco in the mower building, now Virgil Ferris was whining in her ear. The evening was becoming intolerable.

"Look, Virgil." She tried to keep her composure. "You told me the money is safe. You turned it into so much broccoli and then I put it back. It is a simple fucking arrangement. You did put it back, didn't you?"

"I did. It is in the bank. At least I think it is."

"What the fuck do you mean you 'think it is'? How the hell can it be gone? What the hell did you do, spend it? So help me God, if you spent even-"

"No! No! Nothing like that. It is just that I'm not

sure I can find it in my accounting records."

"You better start making sense, Virgil." June could hear him breathing hard and quick through his nostrils on the other end. From all the years she'd been funneling her dominatrix money through the grocery store, she knew he wasn't dishonest, at least not with her. However, he could be rather inattentive; that is, unless he had a collar around his neck. Then you couldn't divide his attention by two.

"It is just... I'm not sure how much there is. I don't know if I can come up with that amount without having to liquidate stock."

"Don't you have your accounts in a computer program?"

"Yeah, but the program keeps changing. It used to put all of the totals in with the produce purchases, but it keeps showing up in a column called 'outgoing expenses.' I'd never even seen that column before last week. I still haven't figured it out. It is like it knows all of the expenditures, matches it with the inflow cash, and then matches that against the bank account. I have no idea how it can know what is in that account. It is like it keeps evolving. One time, I was thinking that it would be nice if the inventory program could interface with the spreadsheet, then a week later, it does! I mean I wasn't even in the office when I said it. I don't know how the computer-"

"Ferris," June wasn't following any of it. Using Virgil's last name always put him in a submissive position. She needed control.

"Yes, Ma'am," Virgil said. "Then I found ten dollars."

"What the hell are you talking about? What ten

dollars?"

"Never mind," Virgil never got the hang of Tiffany's advice about telling uninteresting stories.

"Look, Virgil. I am going to be by your office tonight. I'm going to need to see those accounts. I'm going to want to see that money. I'm going to want to be very reassured that you can come up with it, and come up with it fast. I may have to liquidate at a moment's notice."

"I'll have it. I'll have it. When will you be here?"

Monty called up the boarding house stairs, "We are ready to go. Jed has the car running. Should I bring some of the SuperBalls?"

"No we don't need any fucking SuperBalls. Just get in the fucking car."

"Soup or what?" Virgil asked from the cordless headset at June's ear.

"Never fucking mind, Ferris. You just be ready to show me just how rich I am, or I swear you'll fucking regret it."

"Yes, Ma'am."

June slammed down the cordless phone into the cradle and called down the stairs.

"Monty. Monty, you had better make sure you have the right ammo for that gun. If you fuck this up, it won't just be bikers who get shot." She stomped down the stairs.

Unlike the phones of the Ma Bell era, cradling a cordless phone does not disconnect the conversation when the guy on the other end is the one that called. When Virgil heard June say the words 'guns', 'ammo', and 'shot', he quickly clicked off the phone on his end and turned to the computer screen. He stared at it mentally trying to run the numbers.

He grabbed the keyboard and mouse and rabidly ran through the worksheets with a clarity born of terror. It didn't take long for him to realize that it would all come crashing down soon. When it did, he was either going to get a bullet in the head or jail cell. He had no idea why the spreadsheet wasn't hiding the money, but he did know how much he could get his hands on. It meant leaving - running away. It meant stealing June's money. As soon as the money was gone, it would be only a matter of time before someone figured out the accounts were cooked. It also wouldn't take long for June to figure out where her money went. Maybe he could be in Phoenix by that time, or Guadalajara.

Logging into the store's online bank account, Virgil Ferris was determined to try.

CHAPTER 11

THE SMOKE ROLLED FROM THE VENTS of Lucky's bar, sending the scent of sweet grilled onions and caramelizing elk meat up and down Main Street. Music rolled out in a higher pitch each time the door opened to let happy patrons cross the entryway. Happy greetings of "'scuse me" and "how's it going" were exchanged in equal measures. Exceptional beer flowed from Ralph's taps like compound interest in a 1970's bank account. Ralph could not have been happier. When he was too busy to say "hi" to new arrivals, or wish them safe journeys to those leaving, he would squint a tanned and weathered smile to them as they moved through the door.

Saturday was the one night of the week strangers were barely noticed in the joint. Even so, Ralph knew strangers when he saw them. The man who came through the door around eleven seemed stranger than most. The stranger walked in, moving with the kind of even shuffle Ralph long ago witnessed some sailors do to keep their center of gravity below them on a pitching deck. Done correctly, most people don't notice. This was no sailor, however. The stranger was dressed in tan pants and a matching blazer over a deep blue shirt.

He wore a red and white-striped tie and tortoise shell glasses. His hair parted slightly to the side in a common style. He looked like a rather diminutive and less attractive Clark Kent - or maybe a college professor.

He sat at the bar near the far end. Ralph knew there was going to be a problem when Scott Dobbs got up from the stool next to the stranger and threaded his way through the crowd and out the front door. Scott was ever the canary in the coalmine when it came to trouble. Ralph watched him leave without looking back and then walked to stand in front of the stranger, blocking the line of sight to whatever he was staring at on the wall behind the bar. It was a move of male dominance both men recognized but wouldn't acknowledge.

"What'll you have?" Ralph asked.

"Just a beer," the stranger said.

"Any particular flavor?"

A loud voice came up over the general din of the bar. "That dumb shit probably still has my boot print on his head." It was Bill Ullage from the pool table several feet behind the stranger. "I'll bet he keeps checking it in the mirror every five miles to see if it's faded." Bill and both of the Simon boys laughed, though the latter not quite as enthusiastically.

"I'm sorry," the stranger said to Ralph. "You asked me a question?"

"What flavor of beer would you like?"

The stranger raised an eyebrow. "I'll have what the obnoxious gentleman behind me is having."

Bill continued. "I'll bet he isn't even out of town yet. I'll bet he is still over at Jefferies' trying to get his bike put back together. He'll probably be there for a week."

The brown-suited man turned on his bar stool, rose, and walked toward the pool table. He gently tapped Bill on the shoulder from behind.

"Excuse me," The man said. "This stranger - would his name happen to be Michael Chord?"

Bill turned to face the newcomer, who was at least six inches shorter than Bill. Cecil and Gary stepped up behind Bill, just to feel menacing.

"Yeah, that's the guy. Friend of yours?"

"Of a sort."

"You might want to lend him a couple of bucks."

"Oh? And why would that be?"

Bill moved up into the smaller man's personal space. The man didn't move, which made Bill a little uneasy, but damn if he was going to show it.

"Because," Bill said looking down his chin at the man, "he is going to need a brand new tricycle. His is a little bit busted."

"Then you are the one responsible for him being so long in this town."

"'S'pose so. What's it to you?"

The stranger looked down, moving from Bill's face to stare directly into the open collar of Bill's shirt.

"It is nothing to me, my friend." he said. "In fact, I appreciate you forestalling his endeavors that I may make his acquaintance in a professional capacity.

"Still," he continued, "to desecrate a man's livelihood for the sake of falsely elevating one's ailing social status. Well, that isn't exactly excusable."

"What are you-" Bill started.

With a fluid, feline motion, the stranger dropped, shooting a leg behind him across the floor for balance while driving his fist into Bill's crotch with considerable upward force. The oaf didn't make a sound. He simply slumped wide-eyed onto the floor. The emergency room doctors would later discover that this move, executed correctly, could tear a grown man's testicle into three pieces.

Lucky's was silent. The Simon brothers hadn't made a move, but they instinctively brought their knees closer together. Even the jukebox paused between songs.

"Now," said the stranger as he laid a ten-dollar bill on the bar. "Would someone be so kind as to direct me to an establishment called 'Jefferies'?"

While Sydney finished her explanation of the events leading up to her arrival, the men listened intently. They only asked the occasional question, none of which made sense to Sydney.

"You mean real SuperBalls?"

"What kind of mower did you hit?"

"Was it cold in there?"

The entire time, Jefferies was doing something on the computer, barely pausing to inquire about the mower. He would furiously type out a rhythm, hit the Enter key, and then repeat. His speed was increasing as he continued. Sydney was really finding it annoying.

"Excuse me," she finally asked Chord. "What

exactly is he doing?"

Chord sighed and looked out at the parking lot. Marty and Barry's bikes stood in the shadows beneath a large oak tree across way. When the three left to round up their rides, Chord and Jefferies worked on the flash drive. When Jefferies plugged the flash drive from the transport bag into the office computer, a message popped up right away asking for a password. Jefferies started at "a", then "b", then "c". By the time the trio came back, Jefferies had worked through the entire alphabet to three places. Chord looked to see Jefferies type "a-a-t".

"He calls it a 'brute force' attack," Chord said. "I offered to get him a hammer, but he said it would be counter-productive."

"Wait," Barry said holding the pouch. "There really were no diamonds in the bag, just these glass beads and that flash drive?"

"Yep," Chord said.

"It seems to me that someone went to some trouble to convince you this was just another run. They didn't want you to know what you were really moving."

"That's the way I figure it. If we could just get into the damn thing, we'd know why."

A backfire in the parking lot caused them all to jump. Jefferies didn't miss a beat. The four others looked out the flame-painted window to see an RV ramble into the parking lot. The old lady behind the wheel swerved to miss the parked motorcycles. Rhapsode, his head stuck out of the passenger window, nearly fell to the floor as the RV slid to a halt parallel to the shop. A pump handle and dripping length of hose jutted from the gas tank. They could hear an uproarious cackle from inside the RV.

"Ella!" Jefferies exclaimed. He got up, completely forgetting the string of passwords he'd been trying. "She got it started!" He ran out the front door, the rest following behind. Chord took the time to yank the flash drive.

Ella was already out of the vehicle and standing in the driveway, her hand proudly on the hood of the RV.

"Ella," Jefferies said. He was looking at the RV and back to Ella. "You got her started! What'd you use?"

"Well," Ella said "Since Virgil won't let me buy any more ether at the Fareway, ever since the 'incident' in aisle three, I've been going to the Walgreen's."

"I heard about the incident. It's why Sheriff Clark told me I couldn't give you any ether either. Wait, Walgreen's sells ether?"

"Better. They have perfume. It took me a bunch of tries but I finally got it. It took a whole bottle, but it did the trick."

"And?"

"Let me guess," Sydney said, sniffing a wrinkling nose in the air. "Tommy Boy?"

"No, that only works on the squirrels."

"So what did the trick?" Jefferies was bursting.

"Calvin Klein's Escape. Worked like a charm. She fired right up. I think she's got a little more pickup now too! Too bad that stuff is thirty dollars a bottle."

A bark came from the center of the RV.

"Oh, I almost forgot about your dog." Ellen opened the driver's door. "Come on, boy."

There was a hairy red blur as the Duck Toller shot out past the people and ran under the RV, barking madly. From under the front of the camper shot a smaller streak of red fur. The buck squirrel ran across the parking lot in the most direct line away from the barking dog - straight for the group. Sydney jumped back bumping into Chord, causing him to drop the drive.

"Watch it," Chord said grabbing her to keep from falling.

"Watch it yourself," she said removing his hands from around her chest. "What is it with the men in this town and breasts?"

"Tell me about it," Ella said rolling her eyes.

Rhapsode, determining that the squirrel was no longer under the car, shot out and started a perimeter, nose-to-the-ground search. Being better suited to hunting ducks than rodents, he had a bit of trouble finding the scent.

For his part, the squirrel was hiding behind Chord's legs, madly plotting his next escape run, when he spotted the flash drive lying on the pavement. Now there is a nut a doe could love him for. The squirrel grabbed the drive at the same time Rhapsode and Chord both saw him.

With an instinctive moment of lucidity, the squirrel executed Escape Plan Theta.

John Montét

CHAPTER 12

WHEN JAIRUS AND TIFFANY FINALLY REACHED The House of Grease, both were moving with exhausted, limping slowness. Jairus was following the RV's wild zigzag through town - offering apologies to property owners on behalf of the canine passenger whenever it seemed prudent - before Tiffany finally caught up with him. Her knee throbbed and started to stiffen, giving Tiffany a pronounced limp. Jairus admonished her to sit down and elevate the knee once she caught up to him. Now he was glad she ignored him. He found himself having to lean on her to keep going. It had been a long time since he'd had a decent constitutional.

The pair could see that beyond the overly fragrant van, a crowd gathered at House of Grease. Several of the people stood at the base of the telephone pole in the corner of the parking lot. Every eye focused upward, staring at what appeared to be a squirrel perched on a telephone wire. In his hands, the squirrel turned a small black object in its paws.

"You better not be harassing that poor squiggle."

The party turned as a unit to look at Tiffany.

"I think he's actually harassing us," Chord said. "He has my thumb drive."

"That could scarcely be called harassment," Jairus said. "If he had your actual thumb... now that would be another matter."

At the sound of his voice, Rhapsode bounded out of the crowd. He ran most of the way to greet Jairus, but pulled up short. He dropped his head, tucked his tail between his legs, and slowly walked to Jairus' side.

"Awww. See? He's sorry," Tiffany said. Jairus had told her how he'd woke up from a most excellent nap to find his sole companion missing - no note in sight.

"He's not sorry. He's been in the sauce." Jairus glared at Ella who skillfully ignored him from a distance.

Tiffany turned to the cool drink of water in the black leather jacket. "So the tree rat has your flash drive, huh? How you thinking you'll get it back?"

"I was considering buying a hand gun, but there is that pesky three-day waiting period." Seeing her glower, he quickly added, "So I thought I'd see if we can find something to bait him off that line."

"Nutter Butters work great," Ella said. "Works every time. I've got a sweetie in the RV that ate two of them before she realized I caught her."

"You catch squirrels?" Tiffany asked. "What do you do with them once you've caught them?" She was preparing to be horrified.

"I spruce them up a bit and let them go. They smell horrible. But I'm sensitive to it, I guess. What did you think I did with them, dear? They are terrible canasta players."

"What you're saying is that you have a girl

squirrel in the RV, all spruced up and ready for a night on the town?" Tiffany asked.

"Sure. I forgot about her after I got the RV started. I had to bring it to Jefferies for an overhaul. She's past due."

"The squirrel?"

"No, the RV, dear."

"Hey, Mister," Tiffany said to Chord. "If you want that flash drive back, use the hottie squirrel."

Chord looked at her. "You get her. It's your idea."

"No way I'm going in there," she pointed to the RV.

"And why not?" Ella asked.

"Nutter Butters. I'm allergic." Then, seeing Chord's look, she added, "seriously. I have a peanut allergy that would kill an elephant."

"How poetically wretched," Jairus said.

With a sigh, Chord stepped up into the RV. He immediately rushed out in a fit of coughing. After a moment, he took a deep breath, held it, and went in again. He emerged with the cage containing the squirrel. Instantly, the buck on the wire began to chatter. Chord walked to the base of the telephone pole, pointed the opening of the cage at it, and lifted the door. There was a moment when nothing happened. Then the doe shot out of the cage and spiraled up the telephone pole in what is known to squirrels everywhere as Escape Plan Beta.

The two squirrels looked at one another for a moment, the doe looking the buck up and down, both smelling the Tommy Boy on each other. The buck started a quick sniffing routine that, to a squirrel, amounted to three pickup lines, two free drinks, and a peek at his portfolio. The doe suddenly spun around and took off in her most alluring "chase me" fashion. His advances accepted, the buck dropped the flash drive and scurried after his new mate. In the world of squirrels, it is about the getting, not the having.

Two blocks away, parked between streetlights, three figures sat watching the action from inside a green Chevy Nova.

"Was that a fuckin' squirrel he pulled out of the camper?" Monty asked.

The three watched and strained to look up through the top of the windshield as two squirrels came running down the wire above their heads.

"Why would they be fuckin' around with squirrels?" Monty asked of no one in particular.

"Who knows?" Jed said.

"Yeah, but what exactly can you do with a squirrel?"

June was in the back seat. Through the back window, she saw the two squirrels leap from the power line onto a branch that spanned the street. The weight of the squirrels caused the branch to dip, but not low enough to reach the beige Toyota Camry parked under it. The squirrels were soon lost in the leaves of the tree, as decorum dictated.

"It doesn't matter," June said. She turned around to face the other two. "You know what you need to do, correct?"

Jed repeated the steps they'd outlined over the previous ten minutes. The plans had changed for each new arrival to The House of Grease. The last change had come with the appearance of the old man and the limping Goth girl.

"You head in," Jed said, "through the back garage door. We hold back for a couple of minutes. Then I move toward the front and head off anyone leaving that way. Monty goes around to the very back, near the storage locker, and does the same thing. After five minutes, we both walk through the doors. If they don't give us the diamonds, we take them out back one by one."

June waited a bit. "And?"

"Oh," Monty said. "We gag them when we get them out back. Then we set off an M80 firecracker each time so they think we shot each of 'em. We keep doing that until someone inside cracks."

"Exactly," She was actually proud they remembered the plan. After the SuperBall incident, she was starting to have her doubts about these two. "Let's do it."

No one moved.

"Jed?" She said.

He turned around in the passenger seat, "Yeah?"

"Get the fuck out."

"I thought you were going in first."

"I am," she said, "but this car is a coupe, you idiot. You have to let me out."

As she walked away, Monty turned to Jed who was still rubbing his pinched ear. "You think we should have dropped her off closer to the shop?"

"Naw," Jed said. It's more fun to watch her walk away.

Neither of them heard the door of the Camry

open and close in the street behind them.

As fate would have it, neither Jed nor Monty ever saw the inside of the House of Grease. They would, however, become familiar with the West Watershed Urgent Care Facility. Jed didn't see the hand come through the passenger window to tap the pressure point behind his ear. One moment, he was watching his boss's assets turn a corner out of sight. The next moment, everything just went black. After they both woke up the next morning, Jed counted it a blessing that Monty couldn't get a deep enough breath to talk. Monty did say later that he would have sworn it was Clark Kent who stuck a black soup can through Jed's open window. The beanbag it fired broke three of Monty's ribs.

There was a cold wetness creeping up his thigh. It was a damp, uncomfortable sensation - but at least it was a feeling. It was the first he felt, the first inkling that the world around him still existed. As he lay there, the chill spread from the back of his pants, up the sides of his thighs and he became more aware of the darkness. There was a humming, a buzzing that ebbed and flowed while somehow keeping constant. It took him a minute to realize that it wasn't his throbbing head, but rather the night crickets making the noise.

Eyes still shut, he tried to take a deep breath of cool night air and almost screamed, his mouth opened in a silent cry of surprise and agony. His chest shrieked in sharp pain; his ribs felt broken. It was as if someone had shot a medicine ball into his chest with a cannon. He slowly sucked air into his lungs in a long hiss and got just enough of a breath to feel his head clear.

When he finally opened his eyes, he saw the stars come into focus, the Milky Way splayed across the sky in a beautiful smear. Tall stalks of wild grass crept over his peripheral vision, framing the deep expanse of space before him as if to hold him to the ground, waiting for him to lift himself off into the ether of the universe, the shadows of wild vegetation gently embracing him before that final long step off the planet.

However, Neil Clark wasn't ready for that step. Not yet.

Groaning, making every movement slow and deliberate, he sat up, his ass sinking deeper into the mud of the shallow puddle. Gingerly, he felt his chest, searching for the warm wetness that would tell him just how badly he'd been shot. The muzzle of the gun, the last thing he remembered seeing, was huge. Was it his imagination? A gun of that caliber would have put a hole through his chest the size of a cantaloupe. But his shirt was dry - well, the front of it anyway. He wasn't bleeding, which was a relief. Instead, he felt dust, or dirt on his shirt. When he sniffed his fingertips, the scent was chilling and familiar. It was cordite - gunpowder.

Clark had some experience with shotgun shells that fired non-lethal rounds. These shells fired beanbags with enough velocity to bring down a man at up to twenty feet. Even before today he had seen first-hand what they could do to a person. They left nasty abrasions, but were only lethal if they struck soft tissue at close range. What he saw in the car wasn't a shotgun. It was something smaller, easier to conceal, with a bigger diameter. It was some sort of personal defense weapon.

With some effort, Clark managed to get to his feet and step through the grass to the side of the road above. He gauged he was in the ditch next to the very spot he'd stopped the Camry. It and his cruiser were gone. His radio was nowhere to be found, though his duty belt, including his gun, was still present. The whole thing was unnerving. The driver was smart enough, and prepared enough, to catch him off guard with a fake arm. He was also smart enough to not compound his crime with murdering a police officer or taking his weapon. That meant the driver either didn't need another weapon, or had something better. He also didn't consider the sheriff to be a real threat. Combined with the strange weapon, this guy was turning out to be serious trouble. He might be a professional.

Looking down, he saw where he'd been dragged from the shoulder into the ditch. A square black shadow in the short grass turned out to be his wallet. His ID and badge were present, as were his credit cards. Some of his business cards, the ones he handed out to potential witnesses and victims reluctant to talk, were gone. He thought his cash was gone too, but he managed to find three of his thirteen dollars in the grass.

It would be a long walk back to town, especially

in wet pants. Figuring there was nothing to do but start moving, he put his hands in his pockets and started walking, slowly at first. He was still unsure if he had other injuries. His elbow ached a bit. He probably fell on it when he was knocked unconscious. Nothing else seemed to be in disservice.

As he walked, his hands found the spare key fob he'd carried after the third time he had to call Margret to bring the spare set. He had a terrible habit of locking his keys in the trunk of the cruiser. Margret had teased him saying that at least they were safe in the trunk.

Absently, he pressed a button on the fob. Ahead of him, and off to his right, a car beeped. Clark looked to see the lit interior of the cruiser parked a couple hundred feet down a gravel road. It made sense. His attacker couldn't have taken both cars, and it would have been hard to incapacitate the car in a shallow ditch since his radio still worked. It was better to hide it down a road he wasn't likely to walk down once he woke up.

He just hoped he'd left the spare keys in the trunk.

CHAPTER 13

FIVE MINUTES AFTER THE SQUIRRELS LEFT on their honeymoon, the collective group circled around Jefferies' computer. Tiffany was manning the controls, though neither of her hands moved. They simply starred at the password dialog box.

"So what have you tried so far?" she asked.

"I made it all the way to 'a-b-v', " Jefferies said.

"Okay. Where did you start?"

"'a.'"

"You're joking."

"I don't think he is," Chord said.

"Well then, let's skip the brute-force and try a little finesse. We'll start with a few golden oldies."

Tiffany began typing in the long list of common passwords known to every programmer. It is a known fact that a significant number of people use ridiculously simple passwords. She got a hit on her fifth try.

"Damn," Jefferies said.

"What?" Marty asked. "What worked?"

Jefferies answered "12345. I knew I should have started with numbers."

Tiffany wasn't listening. As soon as she got past the security, a program launched, capturing her full attention. It was a command line program, and it was dangerous. She pulled up the Help List of commands, but didn't find what she was looking for. She spent five minutes decompiling the software with a free downloaded program. It didn't work.

"It's like someone programmed this thing in Brainfuck."

"Language, Dear," Ella said.

"Exactly. It's a programming language. That's what it's called, Brainfuck. It is named after what it does to you when you try to program in it."

"And this program is written in that language," Marty asked.

"No, I was just being dramatic. Whatever it was written in, it doesn't want to decompile. I can't see the code."

Chord asked, "Any idea what it does?"

"Sure," she said. "It is a key-logging program."

"What's so special about that?" Sydney asked.

"Nothing really. They're a dime a dozen. You can even catch one on the Internet like a virus. This one appears to be a little more sophisticated than most I've seen, but it isn't remarkable - other than I can't crack into it."

Barry looked at Chord. "So, why pay you five figures to transport a simple program?"

"Yeah. It doesn't make sense," Chord said. "I would think the information it gathers would be more valuable."

"Ha!" Tiffany exclaimed. "That's it." She turned back to the keyboard and mouse. She downloaded a different program, and started typing a blithering string of characters. She was tearing apart any little bit of code she could get her hands on. It wouldn't be much of a technique, but it might be enough to give her what she needed.

Two minutes later she had it.

"I have it," she said. "Most key-loggers are designed to email their information back to a proxy server. That internet traffic makes these programs easier to spot. This one isn't designed to do that though. It is designed to store the data until someone pulls the flash drive from the computer."

"So there is data in here?" Chord asked.

"Tons." Tiffany pointed to the screen. "Each of these compressed and encrypted files are a week's store information. They go back at least three years."

She clicked on one of the more recent ones. Chord could make out some of it. There were sentences enclosed in-between other words that were, in turn, enclosed in greater-than and less-than symbols. Several of them made him very nervous.

"Holy Christ on a Crutch," Tiffany said.

"Yeah," Chord said.

"Language," Ella said. The computer really didn't interest her. Instead, she'd been sneaking glances at Jairus the entire time, though she pretended it was Rhapsode she was interested in each time he nearly caught her.

"What?" Marty asked. "What did you find?"

"These appear to be correspondences between International Business Machines and the D.O.D," Chord said. "IBM and the Department of Defense. No wonder they wanted these files moved like diamonds."

"That's because they'll be more valuable than

diamonds to the right buyer," June Williams said.

They turned around in unison, perhaps out of habit - well almost all of them. Rhapsode had seen the woman come in, but hadn't bothered to mention it. He was feeling too remorseful to stir up trouble. He was also a little queasy from the Pappy's Rye and the wild ride in the RV.

The tall woman held a gun pointed directly at Tiffany's head.

"Oh shit," Sydney said.

"Language, Dear," Ella said.

"Everyone back away from the computer," June said. "I want you to come one by one into the garage and get against that wall." She pointed toward the workshop without looking. "Move too fast and I'll shoot your little computer nerd."

The wall between the garage and the lobby was only two and a half feet high with ten-foot high glass panels reaching the rest of the way to the ceiling. June stood several paces back from the glass, pointing the gun through the open teller window. She had a perfect line to the back of Tiffany's head. From her vantage point, June could see the entire lobby through the wall. There was no place to duck and hide.

"Any chance the glass is bulletproof?" Chord quietly asked Jefferies.

Jefferies looked at him. "Why would it be?"

Once everyone was in the garage, sitting down on the floor, even Rhapsode, June spoke to Tiffany. "Now, pull the drive out of the computer and put it on the window counter."

Tiffany reached for the mouse rather than the

tower sitting on the counter.

"Hey, girl. I said, pull the flash drive out of the computer, now."

"I have to undock it first. Otherwise it could be corrupted."

"Fine, but do it slow. I'm watching the pointer."

Tiffany moved slowly, as instructed. She carefully closed the window containing the data files.

"Don't you move a muscle, Mr. Chord," June said over her shoulder. Chord had moved up to one knee, preparing to spring at her. June hadn't turned around.

"Yes," June said, "I know who you are Mr. Chord. Your reputation clearly precedes you. My contacts in The Cities were very descriptive when I asked them about you."

"I'm touched," Chord said, settling back down.

Finally, Tiffany closed the computer windows and detached the drive.

"I'm pulling it out now." Tiffany tried not to get snappy.

"Good, turn around and set it on the counter."

Tiffany did so.

"Get in there," June said.

Tiffany walked through the open door and joined the others sitting on the floor.

Keeping half an eye on the group sitting on the garage floor, June reached out and picked up the flash drive. It didn't look like five million dollars, but it could be worth much more. She had a buyer in mind in Seattle. She'd head out in the morning to secure the deal. Then she could work on her building her dreams. All she needed now was for those two idiots to show up. They were late.

"That would be mine, thank you," a man's voice said from behind her. June turned to face the voice.

He'd come through the door at the far end of the garage from where she'd expected Monty to arrive. The man looked like a used car salesman in his beige suit and brown shoes. He stood thirty feet away, empty handed, half a smile playing across his face. His hands hung at his side, a stance that should have been open, vulnerable. For some reason, it unnerved June a bit. He seemed far too confident.

"But I have the gun," June said, a hint of unease in her voice. She moved her arm around to point the black handgun at his forehead. "I suggest you sit down with the others, at least until I leave."

"And should I refuse?"

"I'll shoot you."

"Ah," he said. "Then I'll take that option."

The man began to bob from one side to the other, ducking with incredible agility. He wasn't moving fast. June thought it more resembled a slow disco shuffle. To her surprise, she found it nearly impossible to keep her gun trained on him. In a matter of moments, he was standing right in front of her, so close he could have kissed her. Her arm held the gun extended over his left shoulder. She was mesmerized and she hadn't fired a shot.

Gently, and with a quiet smile, he took the flash drive from her and placed it in his front jacket pocket. Without breaking eye contact, he slowly reached up and took her right elbow. Her arm went numb almost instantly causing her to drop the gun. He didn't bother picking it up.

"Now," he said. "I have one more piece of unfinished business." His eyes sparkled directly into June's. Still holding her gaze, he asked the room, "Which of you good people is Michael Chord?"

The answer came as a fist aimed at the man's temple.

Though he had never met him, Chord knew the man by his movements and his general appearance. This was the man the guys in the business called "Fixer". He earned the name form the way he had of transfixing people with conversation, or even just a look. And he was a flexible son of a bitch.

Chord was right in figuring the blow wouldn't land, so he didn't put all of his weight into it. Instead, he retracted it back to his hip, the fingers of his fist palm-up.

Fixer dropped and spun his leg in an arc, catching Chord at the calves, sending him to the floor.

Chord turned to his side as he fell, rolled, and spun up to his feet. Like Fixer, Chord had heavy training in martial arts. Unlike Fixer, he rarely had cause to use the training. He preferred outthinking his aggressors. It was easier on the pocketbook and his client's timeline.

Fixer stood back, well out of range of a quick counterattack. He was completely still, not attacking, not advancing. Chord knew his opponent was waiting for him to make the next move. Martial arts are most powerful when you are on the defense. If your opponent commits to a careless move, the fight is as good as over. You either start on defense, or risk eating pavement - or well-primed concrete.

On the other hand, if your opponent is suddenly distracted...

The front doorbell rang.

Chord inadvertently glanced at the door of the shop.

Fixer made a lunge.

Thunder resounded in the garage.

Fixer went down, hard, screaming in pain.

"Oh my God! I shot him!" June stared down at the wounded, writhing man. She was shaking violently, the smoking gun vibrating in her loosening grasp. Chord had time to see her drop the gun, a hand to her open mouth, before Sheriff Clark ran through the door and pulled her to the floor. In the next moment, she was handcuffed.

Fixer continued to scream. Blood was soaking through his shirt. Chord ran to him, trying to keep him on his back so he could apply pressure to the wound.

The others were already up. The other bikers were moving, running to find a first aid kit, call 911, and see about coffee. Jefferies seemed not to be present, his face frozen with the shock of seeing someone shot. Tiffany buried her head in Jairus' chest while Ella held her from behind.

Chord stripped off the man's jacket and pressed both hands on Fixer's upper chest, near the man's right shoulder. A pool of blood appeared from beneath The Fixer's shoulder and spread across the garage floor. The wounded man was going into shock, though Chord didn't think the shot had hit a lung.

"You have some nice timing, Sheriff," he said.

"I was detained," Clark said.

"Heavy date?"

"Stargazing." The sheriff moved Chord aside, and then roughly turned the injured man on his back. Fixer cried in pain at being flipped, then again as Clark pulled the zip-tie cuffs tight.

"You're making it worse," Chord said.

Clark flipped Fixer onto his back again and pressed on his wound, eliciting pitiful cries with every movement.

"I owe him one." Clark looked at Chord, then at June. The dominatrix was on her knees, staring at her shooting victim with abject horror. "Keep an eye on her."

"The ambulance is on its way," Barry said through the shop door.

"I'll wait for them outside," Sydney said as she headed out the garage door.

"Will he... will he make it?" June asked.

Chord moved to stand by the kneeling woman. He looked back at the man whose face had now gone a bit pale and quiet. Marty unpacked the first aid kit, handing items to Clark as the sheriff worked to stabilize Fixer.

"Probably," Chord said, "though I'm guessing you slowed him down for a while."

"Red," came a distant voice from against the wall. It was Jefferies.

"What's that, dear sir?" Jairus asked over Tiffany's still buried face.

"I think I'll paint the floor red. It will contrast well with the paneling."

　　　　　　　　　　John Montét

CHAPTER 14

THE MORNING BROKE OVER MALLARD LAKE. It would take nearly 24 hours to fix it again. Campers on the far side of the lake were stirring in the yolk-yellow light, their vacation day starting out with the usual granola bars, rising pancakes, and sizzling sausage links. Already fishermen sat on the near bank angling for bass and bluegill to supplement their morning meal. Some were actually lucky enough to catch a few, though most of them simply throw the fish back. Some days it is hard to deal with fish guts before breakfast.

Two miles away, just on the other side of the Mismate River, breakfast had to wait.

As proprietor of the House of Grease, the site of the incident, Kenneth Jefferies gave his statement first. Sheriff Clark requested that a deputy come and take Jefferies to Kenneth's Aunt's place in Deerburg for the week. They needed a chance to process The House of Grease before Jefferies redecorated again. Over the phone, the aunt had assured Clark that she would do her best to convince Jefferies that painting the floor red may be in bad taste. Neither was hopeful.

Jairus slept the night in the RV with Ella after the

two had finished giving their statements. By the morning, Rhapsode wasn't sure he could look either of them in the face again.

Tiffany wasn't talking to anyone just yet. She didn't feel like it. Feigning childhood, she convinced Sheriff Clark to let her give her statement in the early afternoon. She did, however, get the chance to get at Jefferies' computer again while the paramedics were working on the guy who got shot. Unnoticed, she created a new compressed folder and managed to move the data files she'd hidden on Jefferies' desktop into it (which she had done clandestinely even as all of the newbies were looking, thank you very much). She then uploaded it to her online storage. The cop confiscated the thumb drive before the ambulance got there, so she was glad she'd moved the files before the shots started. You never know when good data might come in handy.

State officials transported a much-traumatized June Williams to the county facilities to await arraignment for the kidnapping, bad-spirited flogging, and attempted murder of Sydney Rollins.

The last word Sheriff Clark had from the county hospital was that Fixer was still in serious condition. It seemed no one would actually miss him. This was especially true for the Poli-Sci 302 class at Northern Illinois University. If a professor is more than ten minutes late for a final exam, it's an automatic pass.

Sydney and Chord stood admiring each other's

bikes. They, along with Marty and Barry, had taken turns sleeping while each gave their statement to Sheriff Clark in turn. Sydney's partners were still inside. A paper sign taped to the outside of the office door read "Occupied. No Tasing."

"Is Anamosa still on your agenda?" Chord asked.

"I'm not sure," Sydney said. "We'll see when the guys get done being grilled by our good sheriff. What way are you headed?"

"South. There is a gentleman I have to talk to. I'm thinking there may be some unsavory expletives involved."

Sydney walked up to him until they were toe to toe. She looked up into his face, then at his chest. She smoothed out imaginary wrinkles in the leather.

"You know," she said. "You could ride with us as far as Independence. Maybe you'd change your mind. I'll let you ride drag."

He took her hands, looking down into her eyes. It was tempting. He found her strength alluring, and she certainly had a figure anyone would be happy to follow down the asphalt ribbons. However, the news that Bill What's-His-Name was already hospitalized with a busted nut had left him with an unrequited desire to grind someone's head into gravel. He was sure Jack Dockage, his original connection, had been the one to call in Fixer. Settling that particular score was going to be very satisfying.

"Sorry," Chord said. "Perhaps another time."

"Sure," Sydney said in a tone she hoped didn't sound rejected.

Chord turned, swung a leg over the saddle and fired up the newly tuned Speedmaster. He put on his sunglasses, gave Sydney a smile, and then rolled out onto the highway. He ran quickly through the gears as he sped away. She watched him cross the bridge, head up the long hill, and shrink of sight.

As Sydney turned to go check on the crew, something fluttered on the ground catching her eye. She reached down and picked it up.

"Huh," she said. "I found ten dollars."

ABOUT THIS BOOK

In Vancouver, British Columbia resides a group of authors dedicated to keeping otherwise sane and reasonable fellow writers awake over the three-day Labor Day holiday weekend.

Bastards.

This book is a direct result of their annual effort to interrupt the normal sleeping habits of the just. Not only were they morbidly successful in denying this author some much deserved rest, but they convinced him to pay a nominal fee to do it. They made no promises in doing so, and they delivered none.

They have my undying gratitude.

The International 3-Day novel contest is a Kerouacian exercise in marathon creativity. This decades-old contest pushes authors to develop an entire novel in just 72 hours. A staggering task to be sure, but it is often a much-needed catalyst of creativity for those that would otherwise shillyshally their novel efforts.

To be sure, this novel did not win the 34th annual contest for which it was a competitor. Nor did it make the Honorable Mention List. Having read the first draft, I can hardly fault them. Afterward, when faced with a completed novella, I could not simply walk away. Many revisions later, I am able to present the first of my best efforts.

I should note that the town of Clements does not exist. Nor are the characters in the book modeled directly, or indirectly, after any real individuals living, dead, or imaginary, (any latent multiple personality disorders on my part notwithstanding). This book is for entertainment purposes only. Any meaningful revelations, inspirations, mental incorruptions, vestal virgin sightings, successful life interventions, insights into the answers and questions of the universe, or otherwise positive life experiences generated by this book are entirely unintentional. Should you find or experience any of the above after reading this material, please seek professional help.

ACKNOWLEDGEMENTS

I would like to thank the folks at The International 3-Day Novel Contest for providing me the motivation for pulling together this novella. There are some truly wonderful and innovative folks in Vancouver, BC. I wish them happy slush reading.

This book, in a readable format, would not be possible were it not for the loving dedication of my editor - Linda Montét (a.k.a. "Mom"). Her insight, incredible writing knowledge, and reluctant willingness to treat her son like a well-meaning stranger, propelled this material from a rough piece of lumber into something better than whatever that thing was I gave her during seventh-grade shop class.

Thanks to my father, a man who put me on two wheels - a place I feel I truly belong.

Thanks to John "Juan" Horsfall for his excellent advice regarding the cover design. There is none better than he.

Special thanks to Shepard, Vamp, TNT, Wild Child, Elmo, Nympho, LAR, and the rest of the RVB group. Thank you all for a continued and never-ending source of stories.

Most importantly, I must thank my loving wife, Michelle. She is my love, my life, and my soul mate. She is also my ideal reader. I knew I was hitting the right notes when she laughed aloud at the first draft.

ABOUT THE AUTHOR

John Montét is a writer, guitarist, songwriter, and motorcyclist living near La Crosse, Wisconsin. For money, he works as a Web developer and computer programmer. He is also a lecturer and instructor of online technologies and software.

He steadfastly refuses to refer to himself in the third-person.

www.ingramcontent.com/pod-product-compliance
Lightning Source LLC
Chambersburg PA
CBHW051922240626
47153CB00004B/1332